Anomalies & Curiosities

AN ANTHOLOGY OF GOTHIC MEDICAL HORROR

Anomalies &
Curiosities

AN ANTHOLOGY OF
GOTHIC MEDICAL HORROR

EDITED BY
CASSANDRA L. THOMPSON

QUILL & CROW PUBLISHING HOUSE

Anomalies & Curiosities:
An Anthology of Gothic Medical Horror
Edited by Cassandra L. Thompson
Published by Quill & Crow Publishing House

Cover Design by Liliana Marie Creative.
Printed in the United States of America.

ISBN 978-1-7356863-7-0
ISBN 978-1-7356863-9-4 (ebook)

Publisher's Website: www.quillandcrowpublishinghouse.com

TABLE OF CONTENTS

Transfusion

David Andrews

It was early evening. John Stiller strolled through a wheat field just outside his parents' home. Golden blazes reflected in each strand of the tall budding grass, waving gently in the mid-September breeze. His mind often wondered about the intricacies of the world, questioning how things worked. He focused on the beat of his heart, listening to its rhythm change as his pace quickened then slowed. He watched as crows swooped with masterful precision, riding each twist of the wind - how they casually attached to the branches of the oaks surrounding the field. Hinting at the impending fall, their leaves showed subtle tones of brown.

Smart as a whip, but something was amiss, were the rumblings John had heard from others. His youthful face carried mint green eyes that if gazed into long enough, showed traces of complexity. Parted auburn hair with subtle streaks of red sat atop his round pale head. He rarely smiled. Instead, his lips pressed together in a congenial smirk, which further complicated understanding the boy.

As John approached the tree line, the sun rode its descent to nightfall, casting a reddening madness across the landscape. He noticed his neighbor, George Stillwell, standing in the doorway of his one-room cabin. This was not unusual, it was his own home, and one would expect a man to be entering or leaving at his discretion, but something seemed off. George just stood there, neither coming nor going, standing, looming, hanging in the threshold.

The sun fell several inches in the sky causing details to fade. John looked back to the doorway and saw George's silhouette – slumped over, slowly descending to the ground. John's interest grew. Curiosity pulled him in the direction of the cabin. He did not run. His pace remained even as he walked through the brush into the thinly cleared yard in front of Mr. Stillwell's cabin. When John was close enough to see Mr. Stillwell through the darkness, he observed naked skin with tiny black smudges moving about. Most of them resided on his midsection, near his stomach and thighs. As he moved closer, he noticed George's rib cage protruding, stretching at his thin, pallid flesh. John remembered his neighbor as a stout man with a large belly and plenty of extra meat to carry him through the winters, thinking this should be the season Mr. Stillwell had extra fat. He should not be so thin, so deathly thin.

"Mr. Stillwell?" John said hesitantly. "I'm not sure what is going on, but you seem unwell. Can you tell me what ails you?"

George, now laying on his side, looked up at John with jaundiced eyes, and muttered, "Boy, I came down with the blood sickness. They say my blood is spoiled. These creatures you see on my skin are leeches. They take the sick blood out."

John responded, "Sir, to be quite honest with you, it doesn't seem that you are getting better. Will the doctor be along?"

"No, son, the doctor hasn't been here in weeks. He only comes from town once in a while. But I got a resource to obtain more leeches. Billy Lancing from up the road. Billy has been to the city many times and knows some of the ways of leeching. Since I have not been getting any better, I thought adding more to my skin would help. The quicker I can get the bad blood out, the sooner I'll be back on my feet, and Billy knows how to find them. I don't ask questions – just keep getting fresh ones and adding them to my skin."

John stared at the man, listening to each word as it rolled out of his mouth, and asked, "If you would like, I could help you put more on. Just tell me where they are, and I will get them for you."

The old man looked relieved. "Thank you, son. I believe that is just what I need. If you would step over me, just to the right, you will see under the table a container. Now, you'll have to dip your hand into the water and grab a few. They tend to be slippery, but don't be frightened if one latches onto you. It won't hurt you, just a sign that you have a small sickness. If it does, let it run its course. It will let go once sated."

John ran back across the field with his arms around the bucket. Water splashed from its sides, a few leeches dropping to the ground. He'd left the old man lying in the doorway without a thought. John was reactionary. If he had an idea, he moved on it without hesitation. Later he might wonder if the old man was still on the hard ground, covered in blood suckers, near death, but sadness would not come to John. His thoughts were tactical, never focusing on the emotional nature of life.

He approached his childhood home, a simple, one-story brick house surrounded by a small pasture with only a few hens, a rooster, and a sickly cow. The last few years had been trying for the Stiller family. His father, once a formidable figure, was now hobbled and frail since the accident a couple years back. The strain of his decline showed not only in the deteriorating home, and the animals surrounding it, but on the faces of John's parents, how they hung with uncertainty.

The roof of the house was covered in moss, green sprouts moving in and out of the crevices of each shingle. It crept through cracks, and at night John would lie in his bed staring at the ceiling, wondering how long it might take for it to eat through the entire house. He would compare the sprawling lichen to sickness, how it feasted casually on its host, and wondered what could be done to eradicate it and how to do it without causing further damage to the wood.

John had many ideas, most of which caused him to act. When it came to the moss, he would pull pieces from trees and stones, and study how it reacted to different substances. He would burn it, submerge it in water, set it on manure, urinate on it, and while it always died, he noticed the different rates at which it diminished. He was never sure of what to do with this information, but it always fascinated him.

Grabbing the bucket, John slid into a small barn behind his home. Once inside, he moved to the rear of the rickety structure. Straw was skewed over the floor. Where he stood was a pile of the dried lanky grass. He used his hands to push and pull at the mound until a small wooden cage was exposed. Within the cage was a strange looking creature laying on its side with pink flesh and nubs for arms, writhing in torment. The only hint remaining of its former life as a chicken were its sprawling toes and claws.

Several days prior, John noticed the bird sitting behind the barn. When he nudged it with his boot, it tried to stand, but fell back in place. It was evident the hen was sick, so he relocated it to its newly constructed stilted prison where he would carry out several crude experiments. He thought of the moss, and how it made the roof sick, so he plucked out each feather looking for a sign of the sickness. When he did not see anything except the scarlet glow if its irritated flesh, he grew confused.

However, the day's events had given new hope to solving the riddle of what ailed the bird. When the old man told John, "They take the sick blood out," it immediately answered the question of the hen problem. What was feeding on it was not on the outside, it was on the inside. The moment the man had told him about the leeches, he knew he had to draw the bad blood from the chicken.

With delicate care, John placed his left hand under its long, loose neck and moved his other hand beneath its breast to support its weight. Laying it on a workbench, he observed how close to death it was. With an urgent motion, he plunged both of his hands into the bucket, pulling from it a handful of writhing black blood suckers. The unpleasant feeling of wiggling wetness caused John to toss them onto the body of the bird. Regaining his commitment, he focused, and watched as the leeches wiggled and fell from the hen. Not one attached, so he grabbed at each with the tips of his fingers, gently moving individual leeches to the bird's flesh.

He was perplexed. He had seen them stick to the old man's skin and did not understand why they refused to cooperate, why they slid off the tender flesh of the hen. He continued trying. For hours he moved the leeches to different areas of the bird's body, its neck, its head, its belly, its eyes, but they would not take hold. John's frustration grew to anger. He needed this to work. He wanted to watch their little guts fill with putrid blood. He yearned for control, but neither the leeches nor the chicken would comply.

As his blood pressure increased, his face turned to a sharp red. Unable to contain his rage any longer, he turned and kicked over the bucket. Water spilled, gushing into the hay, disappearing beneath its recesses, leaving only a few leeches exposed to flail on the dry ground. His eyes then turned to the rusty tools scattered on the workbench. He grabbed what looked to be a dirty dulled blade, moved over to the chicken, and sliced a small crude incision in its belly. Then he watched as thick juice oozed into a small puddle on the table. Satisfied with what he had done, he placed the chicken back in its cage, threw the straw back over it and walked out of the barn.

❧

Months had passed. Bitter winter winds blew through the crevices in the decaying stone of his parents home, whistling songs of isolation.

13

Sitting in a chair, John stared into the waning flames of a fire set in a strangely ornate fireplace. The Gibbon's style carved wooden mantle, detailed with twisting vines and leaves, mocked the humble dwelling, a contrast to the muted greys that surrounded it. The chair creaked with his movements. It was a humble place to rest, one that he and his father had built some years ago. It held together with great might, through many winters of wiggling madness that could only be produced from a confined child with bustling energy. The gritty walls of this house brought a sense of contentment to John. It was the only place he had ever lived, and he appreciated its familiarity. The thought struck him to go outside and gather a few more logs. Nighttime was approaching, and a subtle chill was cascading through the room.

The pungent smell of a stew mixed with the remnants of vegetables, and grains, lingered in the air. A detestable concoction that would only be put together by those who were desperate. His mother, standing near the stove, was cleaning up from supper. She nodded at him with a morose grin, dirt streaking her hands and face, agreeing without words, what John was to do.

Shortly after he had eaten, his father had walked to the neighbor's house to barter for some food to make it through the winter. He brought a satchel of wool, hoping the tease of its warm strands might persuade them into parting with something edible. This had left John with the responsibility of keeping the fire going.

John rose from his chair and opened the front door, allowing the whipping winds to penetrate their encapsulated lives. He headed behind the house to the rickety shelter his father had made to keep the split timber dry. Before turning the corner, he paused, listening to the emptiness in the air. He noticed the only sounds around him were those created by the wind. He thought of life and wondered where it hid in the cold.

Days went by. His father never returned. Lines of concern

sketched his mother's face, making it seem as if she had aged years in mere days. There were few words spoken between John and his mother. They both knew what they chose not to speak out loud. John's father had grown increasingly weak through the frigid days. That coupled with his bad leg made his journey to the neighbors, some miles away, a perilous one. His wife had begged him to let John go, but the man was steadfast. His stubbornness was likely the cause of what led to his frozen demise.

John's mother's health declined swiftly. She sat for hours in her rocking chair, staring out into the desolate white, stretching from top to bottom of the window frame. The only sounds in the home were of the crackling fire and wind as it continued its somber sonata through the days and nights.

Eventually, she could no longer sit in her chair. John would open the planked door to his mother's room on occasion, peeking in to see two beds, one empty, the other filled with a lump of human anguish. He would look just long enough to note a subtle movement or breath. Then he would return to his chair, watch the flames in their fire dance, and comb his mind for answers to his latest problem.

He considered what he had learned from the moss, how obvious external pains could be better identified. He thought of the old man and the chicken. The poor fowl laying stiff as a board the morning after its bloodletting. John assumed it had been too late to fix the creature, but what of his mother? He wondered if it was too late for her as well. On the outside, she had no moss, no growths, no festering wounds like his father's after the fall. He knew it must be in her blood, but there were no leeches around and he certainly did not want to take too much blood from her. He suspected that part of the reason the chicken did not make it was because the hole he created in its belly was a bit too large.

He walked to the kitchen, which was only about fifteen steps from his chair. He looked around, opening several cabinets and drawers until the gleam of a thin paring knife caught his eye. Its pointy tip was just what he needed. It would enable him to better control the opening he would make when draining the sickness from his mother.

⁂

John had family in the city. After his mother's passing, and the thaw of spring revealed his father's modestly preserved corpse, he moved in with his mother's sister, and her husband. William and Anna Vance had sufficient wealth, which enabled John to focus on his education.

John thrived in the classroom. His intricate mind constantly examined the information presented to him. He would scrutinize the lectures and the subpar teaching methods, thinking how they could be administered more effectively. He would never voice this to the class, however. Instead, he kept his ideas for a later time, often jotting them down in the thick ledger that he kept neatly tucked away in his bedroom closet. These notes also included his experiments and ideas from life with his parents- from the moss to the chicken to the old man- and other bits of information he'd gathered from that time. Of course, he still had his private moments where he continued to put his ideas to test. He would never stop searching for answers.

One early spring morning, on his way to school, John walked the street, studying the individual stones paved together, the varying shapes all fitting together like a mosaic. Now a boy of sixteen, his aunt and uncle had been pressuring him to decide on a career. His uncle urged him to join the family business, a modest cotton mill that William hoped to expand. He saw intelligence in his nephew and wanted to use his calculated mind to help in his own endeavors.

John did not mind the fetid air of the city, nor the gray haze that hung around every corner. Even the cold rain that dotted the back of his neck did not bother him. Since he first arrived, he had been mesmerized by the activity, the architecture, and most of all, the different faces and personalities he encountered each day.

His thoughts were interrupted by an anguished scream. His daily walk took him past a hospital. Its thick iron gates, painted black, always presented John with ominous intrigue. Beyond the gates was an enormous structure forged from contrasting dark brick and light stone. It stood about three stories with a main entrance having four pillars and four arches leading to the several doors. From this building, at each end, two additional wings pointed to the street, and John thought that it looked like a squared off horseshoe.

Looking in the direction of the sound, he saw a man being held to the ground by three other men. John's gaze landed just above the pillars of the entry and read the engraved words, "Hospital for the Incurable." It was at that moment he decided what his profession would be, not running a mill, but curing the incurable. As soon as school concluded, he would let his aunt and uncle know his plan.

John struggled in college. It was not because he lacked intellect. Most of the information presented in the classroom seemed arbitrary to him, and impatience nudged him to curiosity. He had heard from other students of experiments that were happening below their feet. This led him each evening to wander the basement of the school. As he strolled the long narrow hallway, he would hear stunted moans and doctors whispering amongst themselves in hissing tones. Indiscriminate words that John could never decipher, but they pulled him back each night, offering the hope that he would hear even a sting of two words that might lead him to what was happening in that dismal place below the classrooms.

There were several heavy white painted doors on each side of the hallway, all with brown smudges looming about the handles, sliding onto the paint. When John brought his eyes closer, he could see these marks were from a myriad of fingerprints, mashed together forming a singular mark. This evening, John noticed one of the doors was cracked open. He slinked closer, hoping he would hear a conversation, or even better, steal a glimpse inside the room.

As John peeked inside, two lanterns flickered, casting playful shadows on the murky walls. There was a patient strapped to a table. A blanket covered most of this person, except for the gleaming head that appeared to have been shaven that same day.

John felt a hand touch his shoulder, followed by a deep voice asking, "John, what are you doing down here?"

John whipped around, eyes wide, and saw Dr. Baggot. He was a modestly sized man with a wide nose, thin lips, and unmanaged mutton chops hanging from each of his cheeks. He had no hair on the top of his head, only rough patches of greyish brown that intermingled with his silver ear fuzz.

John recalled meeting Dr. Baggot in one of his classes. He was speaking on the medicinal benefits of mercury, or was it arsenic? What John did remember specifically, was the doctor's comments about blood. He talked about the research and findings related to circulation, and how he had believed that the cause of most sickness was carried in it, through the body, affecting various parts of the patient. Madness was caused from moving foul blood to the brain. Melancholia was caused from too much despair in the blood, likely from a sickened heart. He asserted there may be a correlation between the separate sickened parts infecting others. He used the example of the madman and how he would cry desperate tears of sadness. He concluded mentioning trials occurring at that very moment that would change the world. John wanted to be a part of it. He came to school, not for silly instruction on leeching, or the properties of herbs and minerals, but to play in the fine sanguine liquid that he fantasized over in his childhood.

John replied, "Dr. Baggot, please do forgive me. I will not lie to you and tell you a tale of me accidentally finding my way down here.

I will say, however, that I am greatly interested in your ideas on blood. When I heard your lecture, along with rumblings of the great things happening down here I, well, I just needed to be a part of it."

"John, while I do appreciate your fervor, I do not think that we can allow you to participate. It takes many years of training to appreciate what I do."

John rebutted, "Doctor, please. I am dwindling in the archaic teachings of the classroom. I need the fine mind of one such as yourself to water my garden of inquisition. I have been studying blood since I was a child, and I fear if I do not receive the appropriate training from a delightful, sophisticated mind like yours, I will fall back to my uncle's factory."

"Son, please explain this studying you have done. Do tell me more . . ."

With that, John spoke of the things he had learned, from the chicken to the other small animals he had experimented on in his uncle's basement. John even talked of his mother.

"I must say John," the doctor remarked. "I am amazed at your attention to detail. You are years ahead of the other students in experience, even if your methodology was crude. I will give you an opportunity. Meet me here tomorrow evening at eight-thirty sharp. Don't be a moment late."

John smiled, which he wasn't accustomed to doing, so he quickly placed his hand over his mouth, pulling down on his lips and cheeks to regain a more serious countenance and replied, "Thank you, Dr. Baggot. I promise you will not regret this decision."

Over the next few weeks, John and Dr. Baggot would meet in the musty cellar. Each night seemed to bring a different soul with a new and exciting ailment. On one occasion, a woman in utter despair was brought down. She had tried to hang herself from a chandelier in her dining room. Luckily, the knot she made did not hold, and she came crashing down on the fine cherry wood table. The doctor told John that her heart was in such a grave state that they would need to implore desperate measures. They would cut open her chest, rinse her heart in blessed water, then directly apply mercury.

The doctor then pulled out a strange device, unlike any that John had ever seen. It had a funnel atop it leading to a chamber that birthed a narrow hose. A small hand pump was affixed where the hose met the chamber. As soon as John saw the syringe attached at the end of the hose, he knew what it was intended to do. However, the doctor still advised him, "This tool is what I use for transferring blood. At this point, I have only used it to remove blood from human patients, as you know it is still against law to put blood into any living soul. Still, there have been times when I worked with animals where we moved the blood of a healthy calf to a sickened heifer and had great success. Today we will be using it to draw out this patient's blood. That should allow us to work with her heart in a less difficult environment."

Patients such as this woman, the most ill, the incurable, were brought into the school's basement nightly. There were rants of insanity, sullen moans of the saddened. John never saw a single person improve. From his many conversations with Dr. Baggot, he knew that the only way to cure these individuals was to give them healthy blood, but as the doctor had mentioned many times, this was against the law.

This led John to abscond several bottles of sheep blood in secret. He knew Dr. Baggot rested after supper, waking every night at exactly seven-thirty. Tonight a raving man named Ben was expected to be waiting on the table in the basement for the doctor. Generally, the patients were set up about an hour before the doctor's arrival at eight-thirty.

John arrived alone, watching as three men ascended the staircase that led to the college cellar. As soon as they were out of John's sight, he ran down the stairs into the room where Ben was waiting. He had been mildly sedated with opium. John thought of what the doctors had lectured in class, how it was paramount not to over medicate a patient. Pain was necessary for surgery. Without it and its vigorous stimulation, it was certain that the individual undergoing the knife would fall into far too deep a slumber, which would most certainly lead to death.

With two pint-sized medicine bottles, John approached the side of the patient. He set the glass bottles on the adjacent table next to the blood-drawing apparatus.

He then spoke. "Ben, I can assure you that your fortunes have changed, my good sir. Today I am going to perform a revolutionary procedure that even the most experienced doctors are too afraid to attempt. I say that medicine trumps law. How dare they impede progress of healing? You sir, are fortunate indeed."

With a tinge of saliva dripping from his bottom lip the man replied, "There is no cure for me, doctor."

That word directed at John sent a wave of excitement through his brain. He felt empowered, as if he had the ability to give or take life. However, he only wanted to use it to fix people. He desperately wanted to cure the incurable.

"Benjamin, I know you have many treatments, but none like the kind that I intend to give you today," John continued. "They have called you desolate, unfixable, useless, but I say damn them, damn them and their hypocrisy."

Ben responded with such enthusiasm that spit spewed from his mouth as he shouted, "The devil lives in my head. Not you, nor any doctor, not even God Himself can take the seed of Satan from my encumbered heart. I will burn your hospital to the ground. Just as I told the priests when I set flame to their holy books."

With that, John set to work. His hands were steady as he plunged the crude needle into the man's arm. He then opened one of the bottles and watched as the thick crimson fluid flowed into the funnel on top of the device. Looking directly into Ben's eyes, John pushed down on the pump, moving the sheep's blood into the waiting vein of the sickened man.

John wondered how long it might take for the docile blood of the sheep to take effect on Ben. The contents of the first bottle were nearly delivered into his body when John heard Dr. Baggot yell out, "What on Earth are you doing, Boy?"

John whipped around. He had lost track of time and was now standing face to face with his instructor.

John's excitement could not be contained as he explained, "I have done what you were unable to do, sir. From our conversations I knew this is what you wanted, but were unable to perform because of lawful restraints. Look at the him, full of docile sheep blood, already fast asleep."

"This is unacceptable. I will have to report you to the offices, and more than likely, the law will become involved. You have no idea what might happen with this man. There have been studies on the effects of animal—"

Before Dr. Baggot could finish his sentence, John grabbed a scalpel from the table, yanked at the rough mutton chop hair on the side of the doctor's face, pulled his head back, exposing engorged arteries, and sliced into his wrinkled flesh. No sooner had the knife parted his veins, did a rush of glorious burgundy erupt from his neck. John stood in awe at the quantities. He watched as the geyser pulsated to what John assumed was the beat of the doctor's heart. He was encaptivated, watching blood that was intended to flow through veins, gathering into pools on the ground.

Weeks had passed since the incident in the school basement. John fled the school immediately after killing his mentor. He did not entertain feelings of guilt. His only thoughts remained focused on the treatment he had given Ben, and how he slept with such peaceful grace after getting loaded with sheep's blood. He was sure that he had cured the man and was determined to continue offering his therapy to those in need - the incurable.

John had a plan. He would go to the hospital that he had walked past many times, the horseshoe-shaped structure for the most desperate. Presenting himself as having just completed his training, he would offer his services at little to no pay. John had always listened intently when Dr. Baggot talked. He was a man that loved to speak, and the many nights they met, he did just that, spoke to the patients, to himself, to John about his ideas and accomplishments. John would take much of this information and barter his way into the hospital, sneaking in right under their unsuspecting noses.

It did not take much convincing. The doctors and nurses were overwhelmed with the sick. The city brought plagues of hopeless souls. John listened to the shrill voices and dulled groans that bounced from the walls as he walked the hallways. At every turn of a corridor was a new song of desperation, choruses of desolation that did not disturb John. In fact, these sounds inspired him. He thought of all the opportunity it would bring him, all of those laying in their sick beds that he would help to stand and be free.

Since John brought new ideas to the hospital, he was assigned only those in the gravest of health. He never mentioned his ideas on blood, being that it was still outlawed and his experience with Dr. Baggot had let him know the sort of reaction he was liable to get if he spoke of it. Still, he was exhilarated at the chance to work with those deemed the worst of the incurable.

As John continued walking, he noticed how the white paint on the walls still shined. He remembered watching the hospital being built, how he saw the final stones set in place only a few years ago. As he continued, he approached a staircase. It was adorned with an iron handrail, curving inward, inviting John into its opening. He again would be descending a staircase, just as he had when he met his old mentor. However, these stairs were different. hey held hope. The new paint, the decorative railing, it all invoked a feeling of satisfaction – the closest emotion to happiness that John had ever experienced.

John, again, found himself in a basement. The walls had the same white paint, but without the fanfare and pictures that dotted the walls of the floors above him. It was a numbing space that John welcomed. He continued walking until he reached the last door on the left.

Pushing the door open, the first thing John noticed was the putrid smell that danced about his nostrils, reminding him of the many decaying things he had placed in a pile in his aunt and uncle's cellar, mixed with what could be described as a chamber pot that had not been emptied in many days. Breathing only through his mouth, John moved forward to greet and assess his new patient.

He had been warned of this man's state. Severe procedures had been taken to better his quality of life. His name was Owen. He was about twenty-one years old and prone to fits of self-harm. John had been told stories of possible demonic possession, but he snickered inwardly at such ridiculous reasoning. The only devil he thought that could exist in this man was one tiny enough to sneak into his vessels and course through his body, not in some mysterious invisible wave of a soul or a magic cloud of terror. Whatever the case, John was not one to argue words. What they would call demons, he would call sickness, and it would be removed from this man and replaced with sweet unaffected fluid.

What John saw lying in the bed was only a vestige of a human body. Actions had been taken to remove Owens arms. This occurred after many instances of self-mutilation. John was told of a time that Owen cut his own hair off with a butcher knife to "free the snakes from his mind." After removing most of his hair, the evil in his thoughts

24

persisted, and so Owen found the same knife, and dug deep into his scalp, cutting away chunks of flesh, hoping to prevent his locks from ever growing again.

His parents had taken him to a few churches, where exorcisms had been performed. There were many trips to the country, hoping that a break from the poisoned city air would free him from his fits. And of course, there were endless visits from doctors and trips to hospitals, but nothing worked. When his parents made the decision to go forward with removing Owen's arms, it was done with tears in his mother's eyes. Unfortunately, Owen still had his legs, which he used with uncanny agility and dexterity. He managed to use his toes as shorted fingers and at one point, pulled a knife from his mother's kitchen, cutting his left eye free from his head. At that point, he was committed to the Hospital for the Incurable – where both legs would be removed, leaving only a head, a torso, and four nubs.

As John approached the patient, he could hear whispers. But he was unable to focus on their meaning. His attention was drawn to the empty space where an eye once sat. He traced the scars on the man's face, from the x-shaped ones where his eye once was, which led to the raised spots of mounded flesh that dotted the top of his head. There were still a few places where Owen's hair grew. John thought the poor chap failed at ridding himself of the serpents, but then wondered, what if he was forging down the same path? One of misguided thinking, one of insane reasoning. He stepped back a few feet, assessed the creature in front of him, laughed off these assertions, and spoke to the man. "Owen. I see you are trying to communicate with me, but please do not waste any energy. I know of your problems, and I have a cure for your ailment!"

Owen, now speaking louder than a whisper, said, "You have taken the wrong parts. You must take my head."

John retorted, "Dear sir, that is your sickness talking. We shall have no more talk of such things for I am the doctor, and you are my patient. You will not instruct me in things you have failed to accomplish yourself. Sir, please remain quiet."

But he would not, saying, "I see in your eyes the green storm. I know what stories unfold in the depths of your tilted mind. I am there with you, doctor. We swim in the same putrid waters. We both know the only way to fix me is to take off my head. So off with it!"

John said nothing. He grabbed a rag and stuffed it in the man's mouth, muting the insane words that came from a sickened tongue. He then walked over to the blood device he had taken from his deceased teacher, picked it up, and attached a needle to the end of its tube.

Now that Owen was bound to his bed with large leather straps, used because his lack of extremities required his chest and stomach be fastened down, John inserted the needle into the man's neck. Without limbs to offer passage, he thought this the most effective way to get the sheep blood into the man. He still had a few containers left from what he had procured and used on Benjamin a few weeks prior, which he was certain was good blood. He remembered the peaceful look on the chap's face right before he was interrupted by Dr. Baggot.

John then proceeded to open one of the containers of blood. It smelled different than when he first poured it into the device, less metallic, duller. As he poured it into the funnel, it flowed slower and seemed thicker. When he delivered it into Owen's artery, he needed to use more force on the hand pump than he had on his last patient. He continued for over an hour, until the muscles in his arms burned from strain. When he was about finished with the second container, Owen's body erupted into convulsions. If he had not been strapped to the bed, these movements undoubtedly would have cast his body to the floor. John watched as the leather straps pressed at Owen's flesh. He noticed the pale white skin turning red around them, wondering if they might snap from the strain.

Owen's singular eye rolled up into his head then ticked back into place, now looking directly into John's gaze. The convulsing had ceased and there was now an eerie silence in the room. Owen's green iris did not budge from its focus, now casting a hypnotic sway on John. He had never felt anything like fear, never doubted his thinking, but this white and green orb demanded he listen.

Owen slurred and uttered, "Thank you, Doctor. You have freed me from this prison, this broken mind, this amputated body. You indeed found the cure in that device, and now I may take my leave."

Owen's chest took one final heave then went still. John stood silent, then turned and walked out of the room. He would let the nurses and orderlies know of the clean-up and disposal that was needed, but he would never speak another word of this man.

John continued to move forward with his treatments. He had obtained a new resource for his medicinal fluid and had a perfect prospect that lay in a private room. It was not in the basement, but down the hall from the dormitory that held hordes of the ill. The overabundance of patients had given John the opportunity to work with more than just the most serious cases.

John entered the room and moved to the bedside of his new patient. She had been admitted about a week ago with melancholia. Her husband, unable to care for her, thought it best if she received treatment. He had bought her flowers, made jokes to cheer her mood, even once cooking supper, but nothing seemed to work. Now she was John's to fix. In thinking of this patient, he considered her demeanor, then thought of the happy cattle that he would watch graze from his childhood. He had dealt with his new resource, the local butcher, in procuring a bottle of a fine heifer, which had been slaughtered only hours ago.

The patient was already prepared. Earlier in the day, he had instructed the nurses to secure her to the bed. Her hands and legs were bound by leather straps, but she did not struggle, only laying catatonic, staring at the ceiling. Grabbing his blood-moving device, he moved next to her, placing the device on a table near her bed.

He then spoke, "Susan, I have devised a treatment for your melancholia. You will be one of the very first to receive this life changing procedure. This device will move the cheerful blood in this bottle into your vein, carrying it to your heart. Once the treatments are complete, you should be able to go back to your life with your husband. This is great news, isn't it Susan?"

But Susan did not speak. Her eyes moved slightly in the doctor's direction, and a singular tear fell to her cheek, running down until it dropped from her chin.

John continued, "Susan, I see your tears, those that even the most ardent devoted husband could not cure. Rest assured those will dry, for cheerful days lie ahead."

"I will explain what will happen. I will take this needle, insert it into your arm, then pour the contents of this bottle into the funnel atop of the device, and then will use this lever to slowly pump the fluid into you." No other words were spoken as John performed his procedure. When completed, he looked into Susan's eyes, now enlarged, exposing reddened veins. "I believe this has been a success. The nurses should be in throughout the night as usual to check on you. I will be back in the morning, expecting a smile on your face. Do rest well, Susan."

The next day, John woke up before the sun rose. Excitement jostling around in his mind made it impossible for him to sleep any longer. He lay in the bed picturing a pleasant smile on Susan's face. How, at that moment, she might be thinking of how much her husband loved her, and how it would make her beam with delight. He rushed to the private room, but as he approached, he saw several people coming in and out of the room.

Of these people, a nurse approached him. "Dr. Stiller, poor Susan took a turn for the worse. Last night I went to check on her and found her lying still with no breath. There were many tears still wet on her face, so many that they soaked the bedding under her head. There is no doubt that the melancholy won. I am sorry, doctor."

After the nurse finished speaking, a man walked up behind John. He spoke loudly, making demands. "I want to see my wife now."

The nurse looked in John's direction, letting him know this man was his to deal with.

John turned to him and spoke, "Sir, I want you to know we did our best. The sadness was too great. I just, well, I cannot tell you, but there are things not meant for this world sir. I am sorry."

After speaking, John abruptly departed. His pace quickened as he neared the hospital exit. He listened to the beat of his heart accelerating and thought of his own blood coursing through his body – then he stopped abruptly in his tracks. He realized that it was him, or others like him, who carried the blood that would fix the sick. Not animals, but humans, even those with temperaments. This had to be the answer and the next question he thought of was how he might find a supply of this fine human nectar.

Once again, John was relegated to the hospital basement. He saw many patients during this time but was always assigned a nurse to monitor his work. This was because of rumblings and rumors that he used unsavory practices making their way around the hospital. He was frustrated. He had come to a decision. He would use his own blood to inject into the sick and wanted to get to work.

His plan was in place. He thought about how he would pull the blood from his own arm, how he would fill the device once again, how he would push his own substance into a patient who should have been peacefully sleeping in the hospital basement.

He started walking the same streets he did as a teenager on his way to school. It was the night of a new moon, darkness expanding in all directions, covering the brick beneath his feet, and obscuring the tall walls of the buildings on each side of him. After moving through a narrow alley, he arrived near the back entrance of the hospital, where he could again begin his work.

He entered this passage, but before he could take another step, a shadowy figure stepped in front of him.

The man only spoke five words, "This is for my wife," before he pulled a dagger from his undercoat and forced it into John's belly. With each thrust of the blade, John felt a hot searing pain though his midsection - followed by streams of his sacred blood leaving him, flowing faster with each cut. The dullness of the night shined in comparison to the blackness John saw as his consciousness left him.

He could hear voices. Cheerful tones bounced around his periphery. John tried to open his eyes, but the light burned at each attempt. Finally, he heard clear words. "Nurse, please close the curtains. It seems the Doctor is waking."

Behind his eyelids, John could see the light dim. He again attempted to look around, this time with success. He saw a doctor standing before him who he had never seen before. He did recognize the room he was in - it was the same one where he had given cow's blood to Susan.

But before he could completely gather his consciousness, the unrecognizable doctor spoke. "Dr. Stiller, I am so glad you have awoken. Many days ago, you were attacked by the husband of one of your less fortunate patients. But please do not worry, he has been detained, and a swift execution will likely result."

Confused and agitated, John attempted to sit up in his bed, but weakness won, and he fell back in place. He could not understand how he still lived. He felt the blood, the mass amounts, gushing from his stomach as he went dark. John looked at the doctor and asked, "But how?"

The doctor offered a wide smile and replied, "Well, John, if you are asking how you survived, I'll let you in on a little secret. I have been working with what we call blood transfusions for some time. Most of my work has been from animal to animal, with the practice on humans being illegal. That is, of course, only until recent changes in the law.

"You are fortunate indeed. As I was taking my leave, I stumbled upon you in the alley. Having lost so much blood, you were in a grave state, and I couldn't waste any time waiting for a donor, so I used my own arm to extract enough to keep you alive. Not only are you the first patient that I performed this life saving procedure on, but the only living soul to share my blood. What a joy and what a day. The marvels of medicine, but who am I telling? Doctor, you know of these wonders yourself, do you not?"

Hearing these words, John laid back and closed his eyes. His assertions had been right. It was the blood of exceptional humans, like himself, such as this doctor, that would change the world. What a waste that so much of it had been spilled on the cobblestone. Still, there was promise. He thought back to the moss of his childhood home, the hen, his mother, and of Dr. Baggot, Owen, Susan, and Ben. He considered how all his research led to this moment, how, as he lay recovering in a bed designated for the incurable, there was now a super fluid mixture moving through his veins. He smiled, for he knew this aggregate was the elixir he'd dreamed of, what he would use to cure the world of its ailments.

Merciful

Cassandra L. Thompson

C lare was jolted by a loud smack against the window, causing her to nearly drop her rosary. Her heartbeat rose in her throat as she unraveled from her genuflection, tucking the string of beads back into their pouch with shaking hands as she left the chapel to investigate.

A sharp gale hit as she rounded the corner, and she tightened the shawl around her shoulders. She moved towards the flower bed to investigate, only to find a sparrow twitching helplessly on the frozen earth. She frowned, determining that it must have flown into the closed window. From the tiny bones that poked out from between its feathers and the way the blood pooled beneath it, she knew there was no hope. Its beady eyes were wide and terrified, a creature unaware that it would soon meet its loving maker. Perhaps it would fly free once more behind Heaven's gates. She decided not to prolong its agony and removed her shawl to gently scoop it up.

It struggled for only a moment, a fruitless attempt to fight her firm grasp before it went still. She waited to make sure it was dead before she headed towards the nearby cemetery. She found a pile of brush next to the infant graves and said a quick prayer as she laid it to rest. "Goodnight, little bird."

She realized her fingers were growing numb from the cold and she rubbed them together for warmth, hurrying back across the courtyard to her office.

The administrative building of St. Margaret's Laundry, formally known as St. Mary Magdalen's Asylum for Fallen Women, was a formidable, red-bricked structure that loomed above, swallowing her in its shadow as she approached the front entrance. She always thought it a shame most weren't unable to witness the beautiful old building with its ornate crosses and statues of the Saints, for it remained hidden by high walls laden with stone. The only structure that could be seen from the street was the smokestack. The smog it billowed out reminded her that although her workday had just begun, others had started before daybreak. She hurried up the concrete steps, crossing herself under a statue of the Blessed Mother before she entered.

The sharp smell of lye stung her nose after her short reprieve outdoors, a shock to the nostrils, no matter how long she'd run the laundry. Most visitors were surprised to discover the smell was so strong in the administrative building, since it was set far back from the workhouse itself, but they acclimated after a bit of time.

Clare slipped into the washroom before heading to her office, wanting to scrub any remnants of bird off her hands. She'd forgotten the public bathroom had a mirror and frowned when she caught a glimpse of herself. She'd never been one for vanity, but she was struck by how strong the lines around her eyes had become. She tucked a wayward lock of hair into her habit, trying to ignore the silver that dusted what had once been a handsome chestnut brown, and turned on the hot water from the tap.

It only took the smell of rose-scented soap to pull the memories from her mind. Every time she scrubbed her hands, she remembered Elizabeth Morely, but the fragrance brought back the dull brown eyes of the ward she'd looked after during her first few months at St. Margaret's.

Clare had been so young back then. She had just joined the Sisters of Charitable Works and relocated to Donnybrook to act as assistant to Sister Margaret, the acting Mother Superior. Sister Margret both impressed and terrified her, and she tried desperately to gain and keep the seasoned nun's approval.

She could tell Sister Margaret didn't care for Elizabeth when her nose crinkled in disgust as she told Clare how the girl suffered from a simple mind that demanded she wash her hands until they were raw. What made her predicament even more precarious were the harsh chemicals the girls worked with in the laundry. Because of this, the nuns monitored her when it came time for her to use the restroom, much to Elizabeth's dismay. She did manage, however, to make her way into the visitor's bathroom one day. And Clare had been the one to catch her.

Clare still couldn't scrub the image from her mind, the poor girl scouring her skin with steel wool and soap, creating gruesome pink bubbles and streams of rusty red that swirled down the drain as she cried. She grew faint from the sight of it, but St. Margaret swept right in and marched the hysterical, bleeding mess straight to the hospital ward. They kept her in an old-fashioned straight jacket for her own protection, refusing to remove it until her skin had completely healed. It took two weeks. Clare could still hear Elizabeth's unrestrained bellowing, begging them to let her free so she could wash her hands. Even after losing a layer of skin, she refused to believe her hands were truly clean.

Clare pushed the memory aside as she dried her own hands on a towel and swiftly exited the room. No sooner did the door snap shut behind her, did a nun interrupt her path.

"There you are, Mother Superior," the young woman said breathlessly. Sister Ruth was a plain girl with a dust of freckles along her nose. "Our new ward has arrived."

Clare had completely forgotten, but she presented her typically hard visage to the woman in front of her, one that would have put Sister

Margaret to shame. "Of course. I will meet her in my office," she said briskly.

"Yes, Mother Superior." The nun nodded, ducking back into the receptionist room.

Clare gathered herself and headed down the corridor that led to her office.

The administrative wing was modern and pleasant compared to the rest of the institution, several paintings of former Mothers hanging along the wall. Yet, the updated lighting fixtures that hung from the high ceilings were dim, causing the older portraits with blurred features to look haunting in their antique glow. A rather large portrait of the deceased Sister Margaret hung right by Clare's office, her beady black eyes glaring at anyone who dared approach her former chamber.

Sister Bridgit was waiting for Clare as she arrived, notebook in hand. She was a small wisp of a girl with doe eyes that gave her a perpetually terrified appearance, even when she managed a smile. She barely spoke, and when she did, it was a whisper that Clare had to strain to hear.

Her arrival came only two weeks prior, when Bishop Martin brought her to St. Margaret's. Clare had been deeply suspicious why he was pushing the girl into her care - she had plenty of nuns under her wing - but he offered an extra allowance for winter supplies in return for her easy compliance. Irish winters were hard, and she never forgot Sister Margaret's warning, "You must apply persistence to get supplies or you will not eat, the same as the Magdalenes." But it was in that moment that Clare realized what he wanted. She was to start training the nun that would replace her.

At the time, she'd been stunned. Had she grown old that quickly? Wasn't it only yesterday that Sister Margaret led her down the hallway, her heels clicking against the linoleum, explaining how the only way the fallen women of Donnybrook could atone for their sins was to work?

That washing was akin to penance, as if the laundering vats held holy water, their stirring sticks like The Savior's very own cross?

And yet, though Clare did not approve, she had learned not to question male authority. Without the compliance of the Sisterhood, the fallen women of Donnybrook would not be cared for, the women and their poor bastard children eternal victims of poverty, prostitution, and disease. St. Margaret's was their safe haven, and it was up to Clare to protect it.

Fortunately, Sister Bridgit ended up being a blessing. She was devout, demure, and had no trouble keeping up with Clare's rigorous schedule. She even brought Clare tea when she stayed late in her office. They'd developed a kindred though the unspoken words between them, the silence that kept them safely at a distance. There was no forced small talk, no pointless conversations. Clare preferred it that way, and so apparently, did Bridgit.

Clare breezed past her and she obediently followed, opening her office door to reveal several of Donnybrook's *Garda Siochana* standing in attendance over a dirty, sullen girl slouched over in her seat. Father Matthew had accompanied them, an ancient man with neck skin that hung like chicken flesh over his collar. "Mother Superior," he greeted her curtly.

Clare straightened her posture, something she did automatically in the presence of men, as if a lengthy spine and the sharp smack of her heels would command their respect. "Thank you for accompanying our new charge, Father Matthew. We can take it from here."

Father Matthew frowned as he stared at the crumpled wretch on the chair. "Are you certain—"

Clare's voice raised an octave, louder, sharper. "Thank you for your help, Father Matthew," she repeated. "And thank you for showing these fine Guards out of our laundry. I'm quite certain they have more important places to be."

Father Matthew reluctantly nodded, gesturing for the bemused officers to follow him out the door.

Once it latched shut behind them, Clare settled down behind her desk, smoothing her skirt underneath her. Sister Bridget settled in her respective place, examining the girl with her typical doe-eyed stare.

The girl hid behind a fringe of oily blonde hair, refusing to look at either of them. Clare could smell her from where she sat, and she tried not to think of the bugs crawling in the poor wretch's hair as she skimmed over her report. It was the typical situation - poor, malnourished, coming from a tumultuous home. It didn't mention whether the girl was simple or penitent, but Clare would determine that soon enough.

"I am Sister Mary Clare, and this is my laundry," she told her. "You may call me Mother Superior. We will get you cleaned up and assigned a room in just a moment, but first, we will need to know how far along you are."

The girl looked up in surprise.

Clare observed her eyes were clear. Not a simpleton. That meant she was a whore.

"How ya know I was up the pole, den?" the girl asked, her accent revealing her lower-class stature.

"No one comes under our care unless they are suffering from the affliction of pregnancy out of wedlock," Clare explained as she made a few notes. The file beneath her wrist would become the girl's permanent file. She had an entire file cabinet full of them; as of January 1st, 1949, she had a little over a hundred poor souls under her care. The thought of it filled her with pride. She might be old enough for replacement, but at least she could retire knowing she had done her job well.

"I dunno when I got stuck with it," the girl muttered. "Dere been too many to say."

Clare's throat tightened. "We do not speak of such things here.

This is a place for repentance and rehabilitation, somewhere to focus on mending your broken relationship with God. You will be tasked with certain jobs while you are here to maintain your room and board. Everyone follows a schedule that you will keep for the duration of your stay."

"How long will dat be?" the girl asked in alarm.

Clare shut the folder. "It has yet to be determined."

There was a knock on the door, and Sister Rose poked her head in.

"Sister Rose will show you to your room and to the showers," Clare told the girl. "You will be expected to report for work tomorrow morning at 8 o'clock following breakfast."

The girl had not looked pleased since her arrival, but the prospect of a warm shower brightened her hazel eyes. Sister Rose smiled at her, but Clare watched her grimace as the girl grew closer.

"Let us head straight to the showers before I show you to your room," she said mildly.

Clare watched them leave, then glanced at Bridgit. "What else is on my agenda for the day?"

Bridgit looked at her clipboard.

Clare remembered being where she was once, reciting Sister Margaret her duties for the day. She wondered if Sister Bridgit would have the stamina to one day take her place. If she had the mental strength to trust God's plan, even when the wards tested her patience. Would she have been able to handle Erin, the willful ward who once escaped? Clare could almost see her now, her toothy smile behind curtains of thick auburn hair.

Erin charmed everyone instantly, which is probably how she managed to sneak away and scale St. Margaret's stone walls while the rest of the girls walked down to the bleach to hang the linen to dry. She'd made it all the way to a tavern in the city, drunk her fill of ale, and carried on with the patrons before the Guard caught up to her, dragging her shrieking back to the institution.

They hosed her down right in the courtyard, even though it was a chilly spring day and the water from the hose was like ice. Sister Margaret insisted it was necessary before she entered the dormitory to ensure she wouldn't bring in any filth she'd acquired carrying on with sordid company.

Clare remained quiet and still as Sister Margaret chastised the girl shivering helplessly on the ground, her lips blue.

"Your beauty is a curse from the Devil," she hissed. "Vanity is a sin." Her beady eyes turned from the girl and found the eyes of the nuns who had gathered around. "Let us take Erin to the hospital ward and remove her temptation."

Clare continued to remain still, formidable even, as Erin shrieked over the dull hum of the clippers, fat chunks of auburn hair falling to the tiled floor.

"Sister Mary Clare!" she sobbed in her direction. "Help me!"

No, she was quite sure Sister Bridgit didn't possess the fortitude to handle such things. She'd actually liked Erin, almost considered her a friend, but she hadn't let her charms work on her. She'd withstood the temptation to help, staring at her as she cried for it. Sister Bridgit would have crumbled with foolish empathy - she was quite sure of it.

"Laura has reached her one-week mark," the girl interrupted with her whispery voice. "She needs to be transported to the birthing ward."

Clare nodded, the spell of her memory, broken.

The hospital ward was one of St. Margaret's greatest achievements. Well-learned, Catholic doctors worked in the adjacent facility as part of their training at St Vincent's, the nearby hospital. They were young, brilliant men, bringing with them all sorts of innovative, moral ideas to assist the women in childbirth.

Clare strode down the labyrinth of corridors into the pregnant dormitory with Bridgit at her heels. The girls must have heard her coming, for the entire dormitory hushed to a dull hum. While most of St. Margaret's wards were already at work in the laundries, the late-term women were allowed to stay in their dorms, performing low labor jobs such as knitting or folding sheets. As soon as they reached one week before their due date, they were taken to the maternity ward where they would remain until they gave birth.

Laura McGully came to the ward an unabashed whore, scooped off Dublin streets by the Guard, who found her passed out in an ally, riddled with fleas. While plenty of girls offered resistance, Laura seemed grateful to get off the streets, even more so when they determined she was pregnant.

"Time already, t'en?" she remarked when she saw Clare and Bridgit walk in.

Clare nodded, offering a rare smile. Laura was one of the few wards she genuinely liked, despite herself.

Laura grabbed her little bag of toiletries and waddled out the door. She ran an affectionate hand down the swell of her stomach. "Gonna meet the little one soon."

Clare held her smile, though she felt a wave of unease.

The children of St. Margaret's did not meet their mothers. They were signed away immediately upon arrival, with little to no hesitation by the girls. As soon as they were born, they went to the wet nurse at the children's home run by another sect of Sisters, raised there with the hopes they'd be adopted one day. It was a far better life than any of them would have without the help of the nuns, but occasionally a mother would fall in love with her child during birth and demand to see it. It was a harrowing ordeal, but it was something the Sisters had learned to be prepared for. Modern medicine provided quick solutions to such things, but Clare often wondered if one day, a girl wouldn't wake up after taking a sedative. They didn't need more bodies in the cemetery; it was getting cramped as it were.

The rest of the day proceeded as usual, Clare finishing her rounds before sunset, but working on paperwork well into the night. She didn't cease until her hands grew stiff and ached from her pen and the muscles in her neck drew up into a solid knot.

She locked up her office, giving the late-night security guard a smileless nod as she exited the administrative building. The chill scolded her for giving away her shawl and she shivered in response, picking up the pace as she headed to the convent.

It was quiet when she entered, the rest of the nuns long retired for the evening. The convent perpetually smelled of incense and astringent, a plain, modest dwelling cluttered with crucifixes affixed on every wall and above every door. The low evening lighting cast an amber glow on the paintings of martyred saints, distorting their faces as she walked past them. It almost appeared St. Lucy had been painted without the eyes forcibly removed from her, St. Felicity's flesh already torn apart by lions.

Unsettled, Clare made her way up the stairs to her room, the only one on the top floor, reserved for the acting Mother Superior. She felt her knees pop as she ascended, reminding her once more of the inevitable end to her tenure. Perhaps it was best if she prepared for her replacement. Who knows how much longer she'd be able to climb the stairs?

She reached the pitch-black top floor, feeling her way past the only other room on the second floor, the chapel, all the way to her bedroom. Her bedroom greeted her stale and spartan, and she wasted no time in removing her shoes. Her feet throbbed, relieved their suffocating prisons were removed.

She moved over to her dresser to light a candle, which filled the room with a muted softness she preferred over the artificial lighting of the modern era. It flickered over the face of her Lord on the cross, a vision that brought her calm. She pulled out her pins and let down her hair, the waves of greyish brown rolling over her shoulders down to her waist as she reached for her brush. She had not cut her hair since the day she'd made her vow to the Sisterhood.

She knelt to begin her nightly devotional, when wind smacked her from the window, disturbing the curtains. She was perplexed, certain she hadn't left the window open. She sighed with irritation, hobbling over to close it.

A bird darted through, knocking her to the ground. She cried out, shielding herself from its beak as it flapped frantically around the room in circles squawking. She watched in horror as the bird ran into the candle, knocking it over as its wings caught flame.

She darted forward, quickly uprighting the fallen stick and smacking out the flames before it caught the rug completely on fire. Then she looked up at the flaming bird, wondering how on earth she was going to save it, but before she had time to think, it flew back out the window, shrieking into the night.

Clare looked down to see her hands were covered in blood, much like Elizabeth's had been so long ago. Panicked, she turned to the bathroom, but the movement released a gush of liquid from between her legs. The red droplets on the ground confirmed her suspicions, but it had been many years since she'd bled in such a way. Was she dying? She wondered before she was gripped with pain that drove her to her knees.

She clutched her midsection, wondering how she was going to call for help, when she heard the hum of a medical saw, the clumsy metal grinding away to the sound of a woman wailing. This is not how I'm supposed to die, she thought helplessly, wondering where the angels were as the black spots forming in her eyes grew bigger and bigger, until she saw nothing but empty darkness.

❦

Clare woke to knocking. She was still on the floor, still alive, the room calm. She groaned as she pulled herself to her feet. She was relieved to note the blood was gone, the bedroom appearing to be perfectly in order, save for a tiny black burn mark on the carpet. The window was shut, a slip of early sunrise peeking through the curtains.

She must have dreamt it all.

Just a dream.

Again, the knocking.

"Just a minute," she snapped. Nuns were not permitted on the second floor unless they were to sick to make it to the church across the yard and needed to use the chapel for their devotions. It was extremely rare for any of them to even approach her doorway.

She hustled to retrieve her clothing. Even though her mind told her the evening's events were a mere slip of the mind, she still didn't understand why she had fainted on the floor and what became of the bird. She attempted to calm the tremor in her hands as she affixed her habit around her face.

Finally, she opened her door with a scowl.

St. Rose's pale, worried face greeted her. Her voice tapered on hysteria. "It's the new ward - you must come."

The blood drained from Clare's face.

The two women hurried through the still slumbering convent, out into the frosty early morning, and straight to the dormitory.

Clare was calm, even as she saw the white-faced guards waiting for her at the doorway, calm as they told her they'd already phoned the doctors, calm even when she saw the night-shift Sister sobbing with her assistant on a bench nearby. She even managed not to slip in the blood pool that had gathered on the floor.

But the moment she saw the crooked wire hanger and the pale, lifeless white hand coiled around the bend, she was twenty years old again, listening to Sister Margaret's shrill, authoritative tone.

"We have to call the doctor," one of the younger nuns sobbed.

"We will absolutely not call the doctor," Mother Superior hissed. "She is a murderer. We do not show mercy to Magdalenes who murder their children."

Clare was trapped, transfixed by the soft green eyes pleading for help as the life slowly drained from them. She was a new ward - Clare didn't even know her name. Her nightgown had soaked up most of the spillage expelling from her womb, her skin ghastly pale. She heard Erin's voice whispering in her ear, *Sister Mary Clare, help me...*

"We have to help her," Clare said, more authoritatively than she'd intended.

Sister Margaret marched right up to her and slapped her hard across the face.

Clare stared at her in shock, hand against her now hot, stinging cheek.

"Even if they save her life," Sister Margaret said between gritted teeth, "she will be tried and given the death penalty. Killing one's own child is murder. It is better we let her bleed out and call the coroner in the morning." She looked disgustedly at the hemorrhaging girl on the floor and crossed herself. "We are being merciful."

"Shouldn't we call Father to administer the Last Rites?" the other nun asked gently.

"No," Sister Margaret sniffed. "She will burn in hell for her sins regardless."

Clare slipped out of the memory, or she thought she did, from the touch of Sister Rose's hand on her arm.

"Sister Mary Clare?"

She turned around to have her call the doctors and let them know the girl was already dead, but the room was spinning, and her voice caught. Instead, she whispered, "Where is Sister Bridgit?"

Sister Rose stared at her blankly. "Sister Bridgit?"

"Yes," Clare said impatiently. "I had trouble sleeping last night and I'm feeling faint. She can take care of this."

Rose put her hand on her shoulder, her face marked with concern. "Mother Superior, we don't have a Sister Bridgit here."

Clare shoved her hand off and marched out of the room. She was exhausted and off-kilter and was certainly in no mood for stupidity.

The sun stretched its arms over the horizon, tossing light over the cemetery as Clare trudged to the convent. She threw the door open, calling, "Sister Bridgit! Sister Bridgit, you are needed!"

The nun's room was empty, of course; the rest of the sisters already at chapel for morning devotion. It was unusual for Bridgit to join them; she usually waited for Clare. Unless...

Clare climbed the stairs to the second-floor chapel near her bedroom. Sure enough, in the dim light of the holy space, she saw the outline of a woman kneeling before the altar.

"Sister Bridgit, you are needed—" Clare began. But when the young woman turned, Clare bit her tongue to stop herself from crying out.

Sister Bridgit's habit was gone, replaced by a hospital gown, her thin blonde hair loose around her gaunt face and doe eyes. Sparrow feathers were caught in its waves, poking painfully out of her skin as if they originated inside her. Clare recoiled, prepared to flee. But she realized they were no longer in the chapel.

They were in the hospital ward.

Two orderlies came up behind Clare, grabbing each of her arms. She cried out in surprise, but before she could demand what the meaning of this was - before she could snap that she would have their jobs - she felt a ripping pain in her abdomen. It rendered her defenseless to

46

stop them as they threw her onto a bed, securing her arms with straps. She let them, consumed by the throes of agony terrorizing her body.

She heard the doctor's voice from across the room.

"I will save you the unsavory details. The baby's head is stuck, and we will have to do a procedure to help the child out."

"You aren't supposed to do that procedure anymore," a woman protested.

The doctor's voice was calm, authoritative. "We must respect the wishes of the Bishop. We need you to sign off on it."

"The women rarely survive the procedure," the woman insisted. Her voice was strangely familiar.

"There is nothing more we can do. If we let it continue, we will lose the child as well. And the child's importance far exceeds the mother's, Sister Mary Clare."

Clare's eyes burst open in confusion, but her eyesight was blurred. All she could see was the silhouette of a priest nearby, chanting a low hum with his rosary, a circle of masked Sister Nurses looking down at her from above.

"Where am I?" she managed.

"It's alright," the closest one assured her. "The baby is stuck, and the doctors need to do a quick procedure to get him out. You do want your baby to live, don't you?"

"Baby?" Clare cried.

"Shhh," another nun soothed.

The pain had reached an overwhelming peak, excruciating jolts pulsating throughout her entire body. It took away her ability to speak, her mind drifting away to memories of when she was young, feeding sheep in the countryside. *Why didn't I just stay there?*

A doctor pushed his way through the throng of holy figures, a long needle in his hand. She watched him move between her legs, which she realized were held in stirrups. Her scream came out loud, wild, inhibited, sharp with terror.

"Hold her down."

Several faceless orderlies came forward.

"This is a local anesthetic. It will help with the pain," one of the nurses tried to explain over a shoulder.

Clare screeched, "What are you doing to me?"

She watched in horror as he cranked her most tender places open, took a mechanical implement that motored itself, and thrust it inside her. She could hear it grind into her pelvic bone, vibrating her entire body, the sound shrill and merciless - *my God, she even smelled the heated bone* - until the pain was so intense, she was gone. She was drifting, flying like a bird in the sky.

"It will be okay, Bridgit," one of the nuns whispered in her ear.

"I'm not Bridgit," she wanted to say, but could not.

I let Bridgit die.

Clare was immersed in celestial sky, the clouds calling to her. Now this was a proper death, she thought. This was the Heaven she was promised. She leapt happily into it, a sparrow soaring to meet its Creator, to fly free with Him. But she plummeted, rejected, falling, falling, falling, until she hit the concrete below her bedroom window with a loud smack.

There was no pain anymore, curiously enough, even though she knew her body was terribly broken. Maybe she'd see some of the Magdalenes as she made her descent, she thought. Maybe they forgave her for all she'd done, saved her a place with them. She saw a swarm of nuns rushing out to see her, letting loose their screams as her twisted body sighed, releasing her soul to Hell.

But the last thing Sister Mary Clare, Mother Superior, heard as her eyes closed and her world went black, was a whisper.

It was Bridgit's voice in her ear.

"Goodnight, little bird."

Note from The Author

While this story is fiction, it is based on Magdalene asylums, or laundries, which were Roman Catholic institutions that housed the "fallen women" of Ireland for the better part of the 20ᵗʰ century. Donnybrook, the institution this story is loosely based upon, wasn't sold until 1992. Symphysiotomies, the archaic practice of cutting the pelvic bone with a chainsaw to aid in childbirth, have been speculated to be used in these asylums up until the 1960s. My intention in writing this story was not to exploit these women, but to honor them by remembering their suffering.

꧁⬧꧂

If you'd like to learn more about these topics, please visit:
www.jfmresearch.com

Embryo

Nick Petrou

An hour before the church abducted Calvin Morgan, he had been on his way home from the asylum and had asked his coachman to drop him off at a pub instead of taking him to his front door. On this occasion, his coachman delivered him to one of London's many King's Arms. He nursed a black beer at a table towards the back, beyond the reach of the gas lamps, numbing himself in preparation for his wife and unborn child. For the latter's arrival, he was less than enthused. Indeed — and while he had only admitted it to his comrade Dr. Shaw — the thought of ending the pregnancy had entered Calvin's mind on more than one occasion, especially when his wife coerced him into discussing names. To name something was to make it real, to give it power.

After he had finished his beer, Calvin began his usual meander home, breathing into his hands like his fingers were kindling. A drizzle varnished the cobblestone streets, and the air reeked of sulfur. He had scarcely made it around the first corner when a carriage powered by two bat-black horses pulled up alongside him. The door flew open, and a sizable man in a cassock addressed him as Dr. Morgan before hoisting him into the carriage like he weighed no more than the sum of his boots and coat. He perceived little after that, mostly just the stench of some sweet-smelling chemical, and when he finally came to consciousness, he was chained to the stone tiles of a crypt.

Calvin's first thought was to scream, which he did, until a clergy-man stepped out of the darkness, arms folded behind his back. By the clergyman's stature alone, he knew he was not the man who had plucked him from the street. This man's features were shadowed, as though his skull were sucking in his face.

"There is no use in howling, doctor," said the clergyman.

Calvin howled anyway, but it was brought to a violent end when a second clergyman stepped out of the darkness and booted his ribs, leaving him gasping for air. This clergyman was of a build that Calvin likened to his abductor. His broad shoulders supported a large bald head with a wax-like sheen.

"You have met Father Roland," said the older clergyman, nodding at his bald companion. "He is my eye — and my fist if need be. I am the vicar of this parish, to which you are now in service. You will soon beg to begin your work, I am sure. But what you must understand, doctor, is that if you should try to escape, or fail to sustain it, we will bury you so deep that not even God could find you."

Calvin managed a syllable before his skull exploded and every-thing went black.

The ensuing days were not so much a test of Calvin's body as his mind. To an extent, he could bear Father Roland's fists, as well as the friction of the iron shackles, but the boredom was the rack, the thumbscrew.

From his corner, which was lit by a single gas lamp above his head, Calvin could only see a short distance into the crypt. It consisted

of a single room with a vaulted ceiling of naked stone bricks supported by an array of columns. Running down the center of the ceiling,
into the darkness, was a bundle of copper pipes, to which his gas lamp
connected. As far as Calvin could tell, the crypt's recesses no longer
housed sarcophagi or coffins, and while the air was musty, there was
also a chemical undertone that reminded him of his laboratory back
at the asylum. The only other notable feature that he could see was the
double door through which Father Roland came and went. The door's
timbers were swollen against its iron straps, and whenever the clergyman opened or closed the door, its shriek echoed through the crypt as
if through a canyon.

Calvin endured four of Father Roland's visits before he stopped
demanding his immediate release and actually listened to the clergyman, who, upon entry, had said, "My knuckles are raw, Dr. Morgan.
We'll soon resort to other means if we must."

Calvin was standing against the wall, hugging his face with his
forearms. "No, w-wait," he said, bottom lip splitting open, blood tasting
like coins in his mouth. "W-What do you want?"

Father Roland's fists unfurled into chubby fingers and palms. "I'll
show you, Dr. Morgan. But try anything stupid, and I'll beat your face
shut."

Calvin slowly lowered his guard. "You will unshackle me?"

Father Roland nodded, his neck fat bulging over his collar. He
produced a key as he approached Calvin, whose eyebrows were level
with the clergyman's top button. When the chain and shackles clattered
to the floor, Calvin said, "Obliged," and started rotating the feeling back
into his hands.

Reversing a few steps, Father Roland reached behind a nearby
column, picked up a gas lantern, and lit it. Then he motioned Calvin to
walk ahead, and the two men followed a hemisphere of golden lamplight down the crypt's central aisle. The chemical scent that Calvin had

previously noted grew stronger, and he soon beheld its source. Built into the back of the crypt, around a stone altar and inside of six of the crypt's rear-most recesses, was a laboratory — as well as something behind the altar which the lantern had yet to reach.

As for the laboratory, it was well equipped, all things considered, exhibiting a range of scientific instruments, including but by no means limited to beakers, syringes, alembics, scales, and microscopes. One recess contained a bookshelf packed with leather-bound tomes. Filling a shelving unit opposite the bookshelf were jars and tanks containing urine-yellow preservation fluid and organs which were of particular interest to Calvin — brains, spinal cords, and other configurations of the human nervous system.

Father Roland went to a panel on the wall and brought the laboratory to light.

Behind the altar, in an area the size of a modest living room, there were eight tall copper tanks which fed, by way of copper pipes, into a glass tank to the front and center. The central tank was cylindrical and reinforced with copper rods that connected the tank's lid to its base, which was made of copper and fitted with valve wheels, gauges, and other controls and dials. The glass contained a nectar-like orange fluid, and what floated in it, hitched to several tubes, was something that at once confused and disgusted Calvin.

He braced himself against the altar, which was littered with half-gutted notebooks and loose sheets of paper. "God. What is it?"

"Your life, Dr. Morgan," said Father Roland, stepping up to Calvin's side. "You'll feed it and make sure it grows."

"I don't even know what it is. I work at an asylum and research neuroregeneration when time and funding permit it. What could I possibly know about that?"

"No," said the clergyman.

"What?"

"You studied at Ingolstadt. Medicine, biology, chemistry."

Calvin's expression had yet to shift from one of utter confusion, but now he directed it at the clergyman.

"Read Dr. Hill's notes and you'll understand why we need a brain doctor."

"Neurologist," Calvin corrected him. "And who is Dr. Hill?"

"He's who you'll be if you don't get to work."

"What?"

"Dead, Dr. Morgan. Dead."

⚜

Over the next three days, Calvin worked to decipher Dr. Hill's notes while trying to stay clear-headed in the presence of what Hill had simply referred to as "the embryo."

In describing the creature, modern taxonomy had proved insufficient. Dr. Hill had assigned it to the animal kingdom, but he had been unable to settle on a phylum. Calvin's best guess was *Mollusca*, with *Arthropoda* at a close second. Either way, both doctors agreed that the creature had been designed for a subaqueous existence, as it lacked the hard structural tissue it might require to maintain a shape when subjected to the planet's gravity. Dr. Hill was even so bold to suggest that the creature might thrive in the vacuum of space, which Calvin dismissed as lunacy along with Hill's *other* ramblings.

With consideration to his more immediate concerns, namely keeping the embryo alive, Calvin gleaned some critical details from Dr. Hill's work. For instance, the various copper tanks were life support systems, replacing the maternal faculties of whatever God-awful creature the embryo had been removed from, a subject on which the church seemed to have kept Dr. Hill intentionally unenlightened. Among such systems was a feeding apparatus composed of a funnel, some copper pipes, three valves, and two organic tubes which Dr. Hill had synthesized himself, a feat for which the late doctor regained some of Calvin's respect. The substance the embryo was suspended in was also artificial, fulfilling the role of amniotic fluid, as well as, in Dr. Hill's words, *"serving as the medium for the vicar's containment spell."*

Calvin wondered what Hill might have done to incur the vicar's wrath, as he had quite literally transcended the bounds of modern science to satiate the embryo. He knew it could not have been Hill's talk of the occult, for he sensed that the clergymen of this particular parish — whichever parish it was — were more than disposed towards such nonsense.

Continuing with Hill's notes on the subject of feeding, it became clear to Calvin why he, and not some other physician, had been chosen. The embryo subsisted solely on brains, of which the human variety yielded the greatest results. Calvin could think of no other creature in all the world with such an abominable diet.

Grasping at least the basics, Calvin picked up where Dr. Hill had left off, using his spare time to ingest more of the late doctor's notes, tend to the wounds Father Roland had gifted him, and plot his escape. His pregnant wife hardly crossed his mind.

Reading about the embryo was one thing, but Calvin found that, as he physically neared the wretch, its presence pressed harder and harder upon him, causing him to vomit when he came within arm's reach of its tank. Despite a lack of sensory organs, and although it had no face, Calvin often felt he had the embryo's undivided attention — an attention that, as Hill agreed, suggested intelligence, even cunning. Calvin, however, could not bring himself to agree with Dr. Hill's conclusion that the embryo was *"objectively a thing of evil, summoned by devil-worshipping cultists who have infiltrated the Church of England."* Staring at the knotted mass of cornflower-blue flesh via its reflection in a well-polished copper tank, Calvin shuddered. Then he set about feeding the creature.

In one of the recesses near the altar, there was a large icebox that housed beakers of human brain tissue and whole brains, one exhibiting signs of acute neurodegeneration. Calvin brought one of the healthier brains to a mortar and pestle by the sink. When he was done, he poured the pulp into a copper bowl and brought it over to the embryo's tank. Somewhere inside the base of the tank, the main copper pipe of the feeding apparatus connected to one of Dr. Hill's organic tubes, which, in turn, connected to the embryo like an umbilical cord. Calvin emptied the bowl into the funnel. He tightened a small valve wheel where the funnel connected to the main copper pipe, then he grimaced at the embryo's flaccid tendril-like appendages, of which there were twelve. "Glut yourself then, filth," he said, loosening the main valve wheel and flushing the copper pipe into the umbilical cord.

The embryo pulsated as it fed.

Next, he checked one of the tank's many gauges, reading the weight of its contents and recording it in a table he had drawn up in a fresh notebook. Since Dr. Hill's "retirement" a little over a week ago, the embryo hadn't grown all that much, remaining about the size of a newborn human baby, but Calvin did note some penny-sized lumps towards the top of the creature's bulk which had so far gone unnoticed. Over the next hour, he monitored the creature's heart rate, blood pressure, nutrient levels, and a range of other attributes, the last being its sensitivity to light, of which it had none. By then, the embryo had passed much of its meal, so Calvin emptied its waste tank into a bucket, vomited into that same bucket, then washed the steaming heap down the sink with water from a hand pump.

Soon after Calvin went to his narrow bed, which had been set up in one of the recesses where the dead had once slept, Father Roland entered the crypt. As Calvin had previously noted, the clergyman always locked the door behind him, and always stuffed the key into his right-hand pocket.

Father Roland went to the altar, scanned the laboratory, then stood over Calvin, who was now sitting on the edge of the bed.

After several long seconds, Calvin pursed his lips and said, "Dr. Hill believes the creature is some sort of demon."

At the word "demon," Father Roland swept the back of his left hand across Calvin's face, sending him to the floor. "*Believed*," corrected the clergyman. "And you'll do best not to speak of demons." His face looked especially waxen — melted, even — where he stood in front of one of the dustier gas lamps.

"What is it then?" said Calvin. "Why am I doing this?"

The clergyman frowned thoughtfully. "You don't need to know."

Calvin climbed to his feet, both palms raised in defense, back pressed against the wall. "You are not sure yourself, are you? The vicar hasn't told you everything."

Father Roland lifted his left hand to his face and inspected the lesion upon his middle knuckle, which had become infected and was now oozing blood and pus. "I know it is of God," he said, "and that we do *God's* work."

Calvin lowered his guard. "If you would retrieve some coal tar, Father, I could extract from it an acid that might quell your affliction."

The clergyman grunted and then left the crypt, leaving Calvin to wrestle with sleep. In Calvin's dreams, he saw his wife splayed over their bed, her skin as gray as the smog shrouding the window. The mattress held her blood like a sponge, as wet and red as a slab of raw mutton. Trailing out between her legs was an umbilical cord, though attached to it was no human baby, but that blasted embryo. The walls of the crypt screamed back at Calvin as he woke in a sweat.

⁘

In the early hours of the next morning, Calvin got out of bed and inspected the lock mechanism on the double door, as he had done each morning prior, then he tested it with a pair of lockpicks he had fashioned from tweezers. But he was no rogue, and his efforts served only to frustrate him. Next, he attempted, using a small hammer, to knock the pins out of the door hinges, but they were of some castle-grade robustness, and he gave up when his once-controlled blows started causing a racket. He would have to find a way to weaken the door, slip out as someone entered, or snatch the key from Father Roland. He knew, however, that trying to overpower that brick chimney of a man was no sane option.

Unable to go back to sleep, Calvin turned on the laboratory lights and stood in front of the embryo, only mildly nauseated by its presence now. Looking at the lumps towards the top of the creature's bulk, Calvin swore they had gotten bigger. He left and came back with a magnifying glass, confirming his observation. After he recorded the change in his notebook, he conducted some general laboratory maintenance, it being far too early to feed the embryo. He lubricated a few valve wheels, polished every glass surface, and then assessed his inventory. Opening the icebox, a cold cloud wafted out and reminded him of Dr. Shaw's research in the field of cryogenics, during which he had successfully solidified carbon dioxide gas. Calvin took note of this too, but only in his mind.

Finishing in the laboratory, Calvin realized he reeked of a beggar. The apron, shirt, and trousers Father Roland had provided him were smeared with grease. He filled a bucket with water from the sink, took off his clothes, and scrubbed the gunk out of his corners and creases. Then he took a scalpel to his face, and shaved, removing all but his side-whiskers. He didn't know how long he would be here and maintaining one's hygiene is vital to maintaining one's sanity and morale.

That evening, while emptying the embryo's waste tank, Calvin managed not to vomit. As the doctor was pouring some of the waste into a beaker (he had thought it best to store a sample for later analysis), Father Roland entered the crypt, a lantern in one hand and a large brown bottle in the other.

The clergyman's nose twitched as he walked into the laboratory. He put the bottle down beside the sink with just shy of enough force to shatter it. "Coal tar."

After spending the next morning extracting carbolic acid crystals from the coal tar, Calvin made them up in a liquid solution and bottled it. Then he tended to his regular duties, taking notes with an almost mechanical detachment. When he shone a magnified lantern upon the embryo, however, testing its sensitivity to light, he became conscious all at once, for the embryo shuddered in reaction to the stimulus.

Pressing his beakish nose against the tank, Calvin saw that those penny-sized lumps had, overnight, developed a distinct texture. Circling the tank, he observed that all twelve lumps were still arranged in a circle, a halo. Then he studied them through a magnifying glass, concluding that they all exhibited the same pattern — a hexagonal lattice. The embryo had developed compound eyes. It could see.

Calvin did not even gag when he emptied the waste tank that evening. He replaced a length of copper piping and polished the embryo's tank where he had pressed his nose against the glass, working the same spot in a tight, feverish circle as he peered into the creature's unblinking eyes, contemplating its thoughts not from a scientific perspective, but an emotional one. Indeed, the longer Calvin stared at the creature, the more and more logical thought he lost to passion, as though he were six pints down, but without the grogginess.

Was the embryo afraid? Did it believe it was cared for? Was it even aware he existed?

Calvin carried such questions to bed with him that night, during which a thunderstorm vibrated the walls. When he finally fell asleep, he dreamed he was sitting on the edge of his bed in his apartment in

London, rocking the embryo in a blanket in his arms, his wife dead on the mattress behind him.

Roland half leaned, half sat against the altar while Calvin inspected the clergyman's massive hand, concluding that the knuckle had healed over well. "You will survive, Roland," he said.

"Obliged," said Roland, rotating his hand in front of his face. Then he turned away from the altar so he faced the embryo, which had grown by almost fifty per cent in the weeks since it had sprouted compound eyes. "The vicar is pleased, Dr. Morgan."

Despite Calvin's situation, which had certainly improved but was still not agreeable, he felt a familiar pride swell through him, inflating his chest. "While the other components of the brain might *sustain* the embryo, they retard its ability to digest the hippocampus and amygdala, of which its diet now solely consists."

Roland rubbed his topmost chin. "You learned all that from its *shite*?"

Calvin, who was now flicking through a notebook on the altar, said, "Somewhat, yes."

After half a minute of silence, in which Roland had not stopped staring at the embryo, the clergyman said, "Shouldn't we name it?"

"What?"

"I was thinking it would be easier if it had a name."

Calvin set down the notebook and followed Roland's gaze. Then he shook his head dismissively and looked down at the altar, allowing his vision to blur. "I assume that, if you could procure coal tar, you could procure other materials too."

"Something with a W, maybe," said Roland. "What about Walter?"

Calvin let out a frustrated sigh. "Can you get them, Roland?"

Roland blinked himself back into the moment. "What sorts of materials?"

"Let me explain," said Calvin. He paused for effect, then continued, "One of my academic peers who I met in Germany, Dr. Shaw, delved deeper into the atom while I, much to Shaw's displeasure, altered my course to become a brain doctor."

"*Neurologist*," said Roland.

Calvin couldn't help but smile. "Shaw succeeded in transmuting carbon dioxide gas into solid carbon dioxide, yet due to internal politics, his work has been largely suppressed. This material would be of great use to us here, Roland. We could freeze tissue more efficiently, render certain storage tanks inert for maintenance purposes, and seize piping in emergency situations. The material has medical applications too, of course, such as banishing warts and skin imperfections."

Roland looked down at his lap. "Warts, you say?"

"If I tell you where to find Dr. Shaw, will you get it? He works in London."

"I suppose you want me to tell him where we're holding you too."

Calvin chuckled. "Better yet, go straight to the Runners."

After Calvin had attacked a fresh batch of cadavers with a bone saw (working for the church, the dead were in no short supply), he removed the hippocampi and amygdalas, then ground just enough of them to feed the embryo, whose appetite was growing. Approaching the tank, he felt no sickness at all, only the tug of responsibility, which it always pleased him to satisfy. While he was checking the valve wheels, he noticed movement out of the corner of his eye. One of the embryo's twelve tendrils was swimming eel-like against the glass, aimed in Calvin's direction.

Calvin walked back and forth in a crescent around the tank, and the tendril followed him. Placing his hand upon the glass, the tendril crumpled itself into his palm.

Calvin's triumphant shouting echoed through the crypt, cheering him on like a crowd. He diluted some ethanol in a test tube and took a shot, then spent the rest of the night dancing about the embryo's tank. When he finally went to bed, he did not think to remove his greasy, bloody apron. In his dreams, his wife had risen from death, and they held their cornflower-blue baby between them in their arms, its tendrils writhing as they kissed and tickled its vein-strewn bulk.

Three days after the embryo had first moved, Roland wheeled a small icebox into the crypt, finding Calvin standing an inch from the tank, hair in a matted shock.

"Your friend Dr. Shaw is quite the eccentric," Roland said as he pushed the icebox into one of the empty recesses near the back.

Calvin didn't move.

"Dr. Morgan?"

Calvin cocked his head. "Yes?"

"The dry ice."

"Ah, yes." Calvin peeled himself away from the glass and went to Roland. As Calvin opened the icebox, a chalky mist tumbled out, erasing both men from the knees down. He shut the icebox and nodded at the clergyman.

Roland shuffled on the spot. "You said something about warts, Dr. Morgan."

Calvin looked down at Roland's crotch then back at the clergyman's reddening face. "You will need to remove your cassock, Father, if I am to take a look."

Thumbs wrestling, Roland reversed a few steps. "There's a service in the church in one hour. I'm on the organ. I have to get ready."

Calvin grinned. "It's not like I'm going anywhere."

For the next three-quarters of an hour, Calvin tended to his usual duties, pausing every so often to engage with the embryo, encouraging it to chase him around the tank with its tendrils, of which it could now operate all twelve. Throughout the next ten minutes after that, Calvin's heart beat faster and faster, until he could bear it no more and leapt up from where he had been sitting against the embryo's tank to execute his plan.

First, he filled a ceramic pitcher with ethanol. Then he took a few dozen chunks of carbon dioxide from the icebox with a pair of tongs, dropping them into a second pitcher. Before he put on a pair of gloves, he pocketed the small hammer he had used for this same purpose in the past. Then he carefully crossed the crypt with both pitchers in hand, setting them down in front of the double door, which he pressed one ear to.

A minute later, he heard the muffled piping of a church organ. Peering back down the central aisle of the crypt, he waved farewell to the embryo, whose tendrils were slithering more frantically by the second. Calvin sighed. Then he emptied the pitcher of ethanol into the pitcher of dry ice.

A thick mist rolled over Calvin's gloves as he poured the super-cold liquid over the lower right-hand door hinge. As it touched the metal, a shrill whistling pierced his skull. But if the metal was contracting, Calvin couldn't see it. He emptied half the pitcher then set it down and took out the hammer. He went to his knees and started striking the bottom of the hinge, trying to knock the pin out the top. His frustration building, he started smashing the hinge at random, hoping it would just split in two — to no avail. He put one ear to the door again, and could still hear the organ playing. Pouring the rest of the liquid over the hinge, he went at it again, but his bones shivered with each strike, and frustration seized him once more. When he had all but worn the flesh from his palm, he fell with his back against the door. Glancing at the hinge out of the corner of his eye, his logical mind told him that, while it may have only moved a fraction, the pin *had* moved, and one more pitcher might do it. But looking back at the embryo down the shadowed length of the crypt, its tendrils sinking in defeat, Calvin was not listening to logic. The dry ice had failed. He would need to bide his time and come up with another plan. How long that took, it didn't matter.

A month later, on the first day of spring, Walter tore his umbilical cord out of his purpling bulk, opting instead to suck his meals straight out of the cord using the tiny mouths he could spawn, and also retract, anywhere on his body in an instant. Rather than gaining color, Calvin lost all of his.

Midway through June, Walter started bobbing up and down and rotating in his tank, having removed all of his tubes except the one which carried away his waste. Calvin ran in circles around the tank, dizzying himself while Walter conveyed his joy by blowing bubbles. Calvin introduced toys too, like sock puppets, balls of putty, and a lidless skull.

In July, the clergy started building an indoor pool somewhere near the church, all while Calvin considered the actual logistics of moving Walter.

By autumn, Calvin could no longer see his mouth through his beard. When Walter started trying to remove the lid from his tank, Calvin had to force himself not to take out a step ladder and help Walter escape. That night, he fed Walter whole hippocampi and amygdalas before eating an uncooked amygdala himself.

With winter a day away, Roland snuck Calvin a bottle of beer with his standard ration of an egg and two slices of bread, as well as a beer for himself. While the men enjoyed their beverages, Walter compressed his bulk against the back of the tank then launched himself forwards, cracking the glass.

"It broke!" said Calvin, shaking Roland by the shoulders. "It broke!"

Roland lumbered away with considerable speed, leaving the double door wide open as he ascended a stone flight and vanished from Calvin's view. Calvin started running, but not towards the door.

He wrapped his arms around Walter's tank, and Walter thrust his bulk against the glass, bubbles escaping his many mouths in violent bursts. "Not yet, Walter!" said Calvin. "Your new home is not quite ready. Not yet, my child. Not yet."

Via the reflection in the glass, Calvin saw the vicar approaching him, with Roland a few steps behind. As Calvin turned to face the vicar, the vicar's lips peeled away from his yellowing teeth.

"Seize him," he said. Roland looked at Calvin, then back at the vicar, who repeated his instruction in a crackling tone that started Roland into immediate action.

As Roland tore Calvin away from the tank, Calvin screamed, clawing trenches into the clergyman's forearms and hands. Roland took it without complaint, dragging Calvin to the vicar's feet then pinning him to the floor with his boot. With even just a fraction of Roland's weight upon his spine, Calvin quickly realized his struggle was pointless. He also understood that Roland was going easy on him. He tried to relax.

Arms folded behind his back, the vicar approached the altar, blocking Calvin's view of the tank. Facing away from the other men, the vicar said, "Marvelous, doctor. Just marvelous. You have done a great service to the church, to God, and to England, which shall finally be purged. Now, what better reward than to enter the Kingdom of Heaven a saint? For you must know that nothing of what we have done here can leave this place. Not yet. Not until it cannot be undone. Father Roland, show the good doctor to our God."

Calvin's brain bounced back and forth in his skull, and all went black.

⁂

When Calvin woke on the footpath around the corner from the King's Arms, head throbbing, hair clotted with blood, he could remember just two things that had happened after Roland had knocked him out.

The first was Roland himself, loading him into the same carriage he had used to abduct him. Roland must have noticed Calvin's eyes open a crack, for he paused to say, "I'm supposed to take you to the woods and bury you, Dr. Morgan. Don't come looking for us. Cross the Channel if you can. Dr. Hill may have been right." Then he shut the door on him.

The second thing Calvin remembered, clearly occurring before the first, was the birth.

Calvin had watched the vicar raise his arms in exaltation as glass and amniotic fluid crashed to the floor. Then, hovering over the altar, suspended by some unseeable force, he saw Walter. Like the shadow of a looming thundercloud, Walter grew, his tendrils swelling in both length and girth and coiling around the columns, his bulk bubbling outwards, flooding the ceiling vaults and sprouting a hundred mouths in a matter of seconds. His expansion was deafening — a clacking of teeth, a sporadic squelching, a rhythmic piping. His reek was sweet and awful, and Calvin could not breathe enough of it. Walter tensed his tendrils, wringing several columns to dust. The crypt shuddered. A section of the brick roof crashed down next to Roland, whose eyes were wide and jowls were trembling. The vicar bellowed a command in a language unknown to Calvin, and Walter recoiled. Then, with what seemed a tremendous effort, he hurled two tendrils straight at the vicar.

But before they reached the clergyman, they crumpled as though they had struck a glass wall. The vicar cackled. Then he launched a verbal barrage, beating Walter into a manageable shape, binding him with invisible chains. Soon, all of Walter's mouths and tendrils hung limp — his racket hushed. The vicar approached Walter's veiny, sweltering bulk as Walter descended from the ceiling. He placed one palm upon him and said, "I christen thee *the second son of Almighty God.*"

With such thoughts in his mind, Calvin now stumbled through the night-time city, his breath billowing out of his throat in thick clouds, his stench frightening passers-by, to whom he clung and cried, "The carriage that delivered me — have you seen it? Where did it go? Where is Father Roland? Where is the church? Where? Where?"

He went from gas lamp to gas lamp, crossing the busy streets without checking for carriages, under whose wheels and hooves he was nearly pulverized on more occasions than one. He was branded a drunken vagrant and mugged for the air in his pockets, and when his excitement tapered, allowing the winter night to take hold of his bones, he curled up on a pile of moldy sacks in an alley and wept until he thought he would die from shivering. As the sky began to gray, he clambered to his feet. Arms folded over his belly, he let his body carry him wherever it wanted to go, saying Walter's name over and over in his head until the word started to come out with his stuttering breath.

Soon enough, he arrived at the front steps of his apartment, the first pale-yellow rays of dawn piercing the smog to illuminate a face that had not seen sunlight in months. He struck the door knocker, and while he waited for his wife to answer, he thought about what he would say next time she coerced him into discussing potential names for their unborn child. But he did not have to think for long. If his wife bore a son, they would name him Walter.

Ill Wind

R.A. Busby

My girl, my girl
Don't lie to me
Tell me where did you sleep last night?
In the pines, in the pines
Where the sun don't ever shine
I will shiver the whole night through.

--Traditional, "In the Pines"

The wind was howling through the pines, and that was just no good at all. At first an insidious whisper, a ghostly tattler of secrets, the wind's voice had gradually risen to a shriek, putting Grady in mind of a woman wailing for a dead baby.

It's a blood gale, maybe, came the thought. Grady told the thought to hush, and it did, but not all the way.

Troubled, he reached for the poppet kept tied in his raggedy bandanna and ran his thumb over it, feeling a momentary reassurance. It was a simple country talisman, he knew, passed down from his father, but all the same, it was a hedge against the darkness. As he stood there on the forest's edge, his back turned to the wood with its grasping branches, Grady recalled the old child's rhyme, *poppet of pine, poppet of pine, forever defend me from thee and from thine*, and shivered.

It ain't nothing, he told himself. *They're asleep.* And close after, the second treacherous idea: *You hope.*

From his position near the turnoff, he shifted from foot to foot, eyeing the rutted wagon tracks picked out by the bright moonlight. The road into Juniper was quiet, and there was no sign of the depot stage bringing the new company doctor. He held his breath to catch the sound of hoof-clops or coach wheels straining up the mountain switchbacks, but there was nothing.

Only the wind.

Restlessly, broad face sagging and miserable, Grady plodded back to the small cluster of canvas tents in a circle near the trees, making a note to tighten the guy lines and check the stakes before the weather worsened. He parted the door-flap and stepped inside.

It was the blood he smelled first.

Even as he peered into darkness broken only by a few kerosene lanterns, the red reek hit him hard, all fleshy and rank as a handful of pennies. Nodding at the partition, he asked the silent woman in the corner, "She in there? Clara?"

From her seat on a three-legged stool, Mrs. Watson eyed him darkly. "Yep, she's in there. Took you long enough."

Ducking his head, Grady removed his battered felt hat and held it, fingers worrying the brim. "Sorry, ma'am. Mrs. Watson, I mean. I only—"

"Shit, Grady, I'm not going to bite. Sit the hell down."

He looked at her, unsure. Stocky and powerful, with a bent-knee tread like the bears he'd grown up with in Virginia, the woman did look capable of biting.

With a sigh, she reached into her bodice, drew out a drawstring tobacco bag, and twisted up a cigarette between her fingers. "You want a cig?" Without waiting for his reply, she flipped one to him, and he caught it.

As he drew on his smoke, Grady glanced once more at the partition. Behind it, he could hear the woman stirring restlessly as she lay on the camp bed, a fold-out identical to those in the five other tents. Mrs. Watson had bought those beds from Mr. Hodges' Mercantile Emporium in town along with a half-dozen washstands, basins, blankets, and six wood chests for the ladies' clothes. *Probably easier. That way they won't have nothing to fight over, I guess.*

The gale rose with a gust and tore away the pine poppet that someone, perhaps Clara herself, had tied to the doorpost as a ward against the evil from the forest. *Didn't work,* Grady reflected, then corrected himself. *Might not be what you're fearing. Might be something else. Tainted water. Moldy meat. Her sickness ain't got nothing to do with the wind. Not a god-damn thing.* He gestured toward the partition. "So is Clara—I mean, how is she, ma'am?"

Without answering him immediately, Mrs. Watson stuck her head behind the canvas flap and peered at the woman on the bed for a long moment before sitting back on the stool and patiently rolling another cigarette. "My hopes, as you might say, aren't real high. Did that doc finally get here?"

Grady twisted his hat once more. His eyes, warm and brown as a hound's, flickered uncomfortably from the dusty toes of Mrs. Watson's leather boots to the ties holding the partition closed. "No'm. Been keeping my eyeballs peeled for it, but the depot stage ain't come. Not yet, anyway."

When Mrs. Watson did not reply, he shifted on his feet, brow furrowing as he spoke. "So—ah. Since the doctor ain't here, I'm not sure what good I could do for you or for poor Clara in the—" He paused, the tattered fringes of his moustache slumping sadly to his chin, then found a word. "In the condition she's in, I mean to say."

Over the glow of her cigarette, Mrs. Watson's eyes shone cold and blue. "Why, you're here to bury her, Grady," she remarked quietly. "That's why I called you down."

He looked down at his feet in quiet protest. "But the doc—"

"He ain't here. And unless he's a goddamned miracle worker, it ain't going to matter anyhow. Ever since they found her, she's just got worse. Easy to see which way the wind's blowing." For a moment they sat in silence, listening to the gusts outside.

Mrs. Watson continued. "When all is said and done, you'll wrap her in her blanket and find somewhere folks don't go. In the forest, maybe. There you'll dig her a nice, deep hole. I even bought a shovel and a pick." She nodded toward the corner where the tools lay. "With those goddamned limestone rocks all over this mountain, you'll need 'em."

"She's asleep?" Grady whispered. "She can't hear us none?"

"Huh. After twenty drops of what I gave her, she wouldn't hear Jesus himself if he hollered in her ear. I notice she's thrashing, though. No sense in her overhearing this, but even so, it's got to be talked through."

"She's not to be buried in the churchyard?" Grady's moustache dipped lower. He glanced up anxiously at the scream of the gale. *Does sound like a baby. Or a woman lookin' for one. Forever defend me from thee and from thine.*

Mrs. Watson snorted. "Where else? You reckon the good towns-folk of Juniper will cede one single mite of church-ground to my girls? Or to me?" She waved a hand. "Don't bet on it. No, it has to be in the forest." At his baleful glance, the woman shook her head. "And don't give me your backwater foolishness about the trees and the wind or whatnot. It'll have to be there."

"She deserves a fair Christian burial," Grady muttered unhappily.

Mrs. Watson's expression softened. "She deserves some kinda burial, fair or foul. I know you'll do right by her. You'll dig the hole, say the nice words, and no one need be the wiser."

"But why we gotta—"

Mrs. Watson held up a hand. "You want town folks panicking? Saying there's sickness out here? A spreading illness, perhaps?" She snorted. "I haven't been here a year, and even I know how bad that'd be. Hell, I'd rather they believe the girls all caught the clap."

The blast rose, shuddering the tent and plucking like an importunate caller at the entrance. At the sound, they both fell silent once again.

"It's whispering," said Grady. "I can almost make out words in it. Can't you too, ma'am?"

Her head snapped around. "No," she declared. "Stop with that folderol, I said. I don't hear squat. Neither do you, and don't be saying otherwise to folks."

He swallowed. "Ma'am, I'm just thinking it's—"

"It's wind. Nothing more. It's from wherever the fuck wind is from. That's a bottom fact. Don't be making trouble where there is none."

From behind the partition, they heard a weak moan, and Grady turned to the slit in the canvas, his face drooping and miserable. "So what do I tell folks if—"

"As far as the town's concerned, you drove Miss Clara to the depot so she could get on home to her mama before the winter, and you ain't seen her since. No reason you should." Digging into her bodice, Mrs. Watson withdrew a damp ten-dollar note. "For your extra trouble." With a nod, she handed it over.

He examined it. Below the words THE UNITED STATES OF AMERICA were twin portraits of Lewis and Clark bookending a buffalo, a beast whose broad shoulders bunched as if to charge with sudden animal ferocity at the red Roman "X" to his right. Its tail was raised defiantly as if to shit on the great scarlet seal of the U.S. Treasury. Its eyes were implacable and cruel, and its justice was patient.

Unsettled, Grady folded the money, hiding the buffalo, and squirreled the bill away in his vest. *Stirring things up. All those exploring sonsabitches. Lewis and Clark. Dan'l Boone. Fuckin' Henry Comstock and all the others out West with their wagons and picks and guns, wrenching things from the earth that shoulda stayed sleeping below like they done before the mountains was even born. They dug too deep out here. Woke up the old things. Shoulda let 'em lie.*

And then something occurred to him that hadn't before, and Grady silently cursed himself for a fool. *Maybe burying her in the forest is all for the better, then. Could be. Like Mama said, it's an ill wind that blows nobody any good.*

The tent quivered harder as the tempest rose, and again he hoped he'd staked the lines taut enough, or they'd all go spinning off to Oz.

Then the screaming began.

Clara lay on the canvas floor, white blanket twisted about her legs like a worm. Even with the dim lantern, Grady could see her face was grotesquely distended, swollen at the throat, the tendons in her neck stiff as harp strings. His second impression was that the woman might simply explode in a hail of blood.

And then she did.

From her mouth, a jet of dark gore splashed onto Grady's tongue, warm and intimate. He tasted pennies, pennies and something darker, almost sweet. With an animal cry, he stumbled backward, scrubbing his hands over his lips, his cheeks pulled down in a tragic mask.

The woman's legs kicked out and out and out, jolted as if from some galvanic force that bent her back like a longbow and whipped her forward with a jolt. The dark spray from her throat splashed across Mrs. Watson's dingy shirtwaist, looking black in the dim lamplight. Grady saw one thick drop hit the washstand and slide down the side of a yellowish bottle reading "Brixton's Neuralgia Mixture."

"She's havin' some kinda fit," he yelled over the roaring, cacophonic bedlam of the woman's screams, his hands scrabbling over her shoulders as he tried to hold her still. "God damn it!" he cried.

"God," Mrs. Watson replied flatly. "Or something else."

With a grunt, Grady whipped the leather belt from his sagging pants and shoved it between Clara's teeth for her to bite on, but her mouth only screamed rancid blood, hands clawing at her stomach around the taut, wet ball that coiled and rose from beneath the tattered fabric of her nightgown. *Jesus, she's exploding. She's simply exploding.*

To his horror, she curled her feet underneath herself, the tangled blanket falling free, and pushed herself upright, staggering like a foal. As he stared at her, the thin muslin nightdress stretched across her abdomen, which swelled and throbbed as if the horrendous thing below her skin was eating her.

There was a small pop. Then came another spattering gush, and a drop hit the kerosene lamp, sizzling there. With a jolt, Clara whipped backward onto the floor, her pelvis undulating in a horrid parody of copulation before her belly burst beneath her hands, blowing out a quivering horde of moving forms that Grady's mind refused to understand at first except as *maggot maggot o god she's full of maggot.*

He staggered outside, stopping only when his shoulder slammed into an unresisting pine trunk and he spun out, nearly falling. Grady sobbed and clutched the tree, gushing out his meal onto the dried brown needles below his feet, his fingers scrabbling across his lips as the words *maggot maggot maggot* refused to leave his mind.

And the other idea, hot on the heels of the first one.

Ill wind. Ill wind. They shoulda let things lie.

⚜

Letter, September 29, 1904, from Dr. Alfred Middleton to Mr. Frank Poole:

...I admit I fell asleep in the carriage, Frank, lulled to troubled unconsciousness by the relentless rocking up the steep mountain passes from the depot, and it was during this ride I had a rather disturbing dream.

In the nightmare—for so I must properly call it--I found myself on a long road embedded between limestone embankments studded with juniper trees. At the sight, my marrow turned all "Zero at the Bone," as Miss Dickinson expressed it, and my breath came in staggering pants. My only thought was the recurring idea, "The roots are cruel. The roots are cruel. They are...awake." Even now, the thought makes me shudder, and I have no idea what it could mean.

On this road a few yards ahead strode a young man in formal mourning, his steps cold and deliberate as if I had affronted him or perhaps caused his grief. And I knew, Frank, though this youth did not turn around, that it was Jude.

I cried out for him, my own dear son, but the rising wind from those sinister, sentient trees shoved the sound back in my throat. I broke into a run, stumbling after him and begging him to stop, stop the carriage, let the doctor out, for there was sickness in the pines.

As I came close enough to grasp Jude by the shoulders, I saw his head whip around with a sudden, sickening jolt to face me fully backwards on a neck impossibly twisted, while his body—ah, God, I can scarcely bear it—continued the same implacable stride forward.

His eyes rolled up then, Frank, showing the whites below, two rotten eggs, sickly and corrupted, with tiny black points fixed on me with an expression of high and sparkling glee.

And he was grinning. So very wide. So many teeth.

"In the pines, in the pines, where the sun don't ever shine," said Jude through those fangs, pointed as a mouthful of knives. "I will shiver the whole night through."

I jerked awake, hearing some noise from without the vehicle, and, tapping my cane on the coach roof, I demanded to know where we were. From the shadowed trees, I saw a burly shape break from the shadows and rush toward us, bellowing as he came to stop.

In my sudden apprehension, the after-effect of my unhallowed dreams, I nearly ordered the coachman to whip the horses hard for the final mile to Juniper, but I am glad I did not do so, and the driver, wiser than I, was already pulling the carriage to a stop.

The rough fellow inquired whether the doctor was within, and at this, I thrust my head through the window and introduced myself as Dr. Alfred Middleton, asking if someone had taken ill, as I had been brought here for that purpose by the board of Old Stone Mining. And as the man told of a sudden sickness in the tents—one he could not or would not describe—the idea came to me once more unbidden: The roots are awake.

The rattletrap noise from the coach faded away, horses' hooves echoing against the limestone embankments. Squaring his shoulders, Dr. Middleton clapped his hat upon his head and held it down to thwart the gusts plucking playfully at the edges of his coat as if to rip it from him.

He picked through a dry ditch filled with hard-edged rock and pine needles, shoes slipping on the uncertain surface. Ahead was the one whose name was evidently Grady, walking at a pace the doctor could not match. His leather medical case thumped uncomfortably on the side of his knee as he followed as swiftly as he was able.

They were coming near the woods. He walked faster, hastening toward the shivering walls of the tents he could see in the moonlight, illuminated from within so the structures glowed an unnatural white against the shadow. Above, the junipers whispered dark conspiracies, and deep inside the forest, the doctor caught a sound that put him in mind of a baby wailing. It must surely be the wind. No child could weather this tempest, he thought, and wished he had remembered his scarf.

"Grady!" cried a rough voice from within the tent. "Where the hell'd you steal off to? Get in here and help me with this, you chicken-hearted fool!"

With a grunt, the large man stumbled up the last short rise and disappeared behind the canvas.

Letter, September 29, 1904, from Dr. Alfred Middleton to Mr. Frank Poole:

... and on my way inside after the chicken-hearted Grady, I stepped on some object I assumed was a rock of some sort, but it appeared to be a doll crafted from pine needles with a twisted red ribbon about its neck. An odd little folk-token I am sure you would appreciate, Frank, being half a pagan yourself. As for me, I have yet to see the scientific study proving the efficacy of such talismans, so I set it aside as a thing of no importance.

Pushing back the door-flap, I observed an ursine, brooding figure in the corner who turned warily to the door as I came in. It was a woman, I saw, a person of about forty or fifty, stout-armed, with coal-black hair gone white at the roots.

She glared up at me with a dull weariness one rarely sees outside a combat field hospital and flicked her hand at me. "Go on outta here. C'mon back tomorrow. The girls ain't open for business right now, mister, and this tent's closed up for the evening, in case you can't tell. Jesus."

I was quite taken aback, Frank, as you may be sure, and it took a moment to collect myself. "I am not here for—" I paused delicately, then pressed on. "For your...services."

She gave a grim, barking laugh. "My 'services'? Look at you, putting on airs. This place ain't nothing but a canvas cathouse, Lord Fancy."

Blinking rapidly, I straightened my spine. "I regret the misunderstanding, madam. Please let me introduce myself. My name is Dr. Alfred Middleton. I am in the employ of Old Stone Mining as a physician. Is there someone here requiring medical attention?" I lifted my bag, somewhat unnecessarily, as a bona fide testifying to my professional acumen, but she gave it only the most cursory glance. "On the drive past this place, the coachman and I heard someone screaming," I added. "We were hailed to a stop by a Mr. Grady, who met us by chance."

"No such thing as chance." She passed a hand over her broad face. "You came too late, Doc. Not your fault. Not that there was anything you could have done about it even if all the devils of Hell had nipped at your heels from the moment you left the depot. Nothing more to do than wait for Grady to come back from town with a cart so's he can carry out the remains. My name's Mrs. Watson, by the way."

Risking the sobriquet 'Lord Fancy' once more, I gave a formal bow and extended my hand, but she waved it aside, not unkindly. "My hand's not one you really want to touch, Doc. Least not till I've had myself a wash."

Now that the door-flap had fallen down, the rising scent within the place hit me, Frank. Subtle at first, like the earth near the creek behind your house in Des Plaines, but beneath it lurked the tang of iron, and the heavy, meaty odor of human flesh.

I made for the partition, but the woman rose with a speed impressive for someone so powerfully built and said, "No, Doc. Just turn back and go your ways. Grady'll take you into town, and you can attend to your business as usual. This never happened."

"Ma'am—Mrs. Watson, if there's a patient who requires my assistance, do allow me to assure you, I consider it my professional duty to assist this person in any way I may do so—"

She broke in. "Well, do allow me to assure you right on back that there's not a goddamn thing to be done. I ain't a doctor, but I can tell dead."

Before her expression returned to what I suspect was its customary hardness, Frank, I saw something rather unexpected. She let slip a small flicker of concern between her eyebrows, and I understood at that moment this formidable figure was afraid.

I nodded. "Why don't you explain the matter to me, Mrs. Watson." I spoke gently and stepped away from the partition. As we did, I noticed the woman's shirtwaist was smeared with a dark substance resembling blood, though I could not be certain in the poor light.

"Sit on down, Doc." She nodded. "You smoke?"

"I fear I do not."

She gave a coughing laugh. "Might want to start." At this, she deftly spun herself a cigarette, and truth to tell, the smoke was indeed a welcome change, disguising the tangy odor from blood and human waste. The woman looked at me sharply as if making an abrupt decision.

"Very well," she relented, gesturing toward the partition. "Take yourself a look. I believe Grady's hightailed it out the back, so no one's there but her. What used to be her, anyway."

The interior was an abattoir. On the floor wrapped in a white wool blanket lay a long shape Dr. Middleton assumed was a body, at least to judge by the spattered blood and flesh blown onto the canvas walls.

"Was this a suicide?" He frowned, staring at the red stains. "A shooting? We heard screaming, but no—no sound of any gunfire."

"No," Mrs. Watson replied, and said no more.

The doctor took a quick step and knelt, turning the bundle over. "Light, please," he gestured brusquely. "If you will, ma'am. Thank you. Here. Shine it on the body, right there. Yes. What was it this lady died of?"

"You mean besides that hole in her belly?" She held aloft the lantern.

Unrolling the canvas, the doctor caught a wave of heavy scent. At first it was flowery, like orange eau-de-cologne or Florida water soured in the folds of flesh. Then it hit, gagging him with its rank, putrescent stench. He backed away, and in the same moment, Mrs. Watson clapped her hands to her face with a hard smack.

The thing in the bundle had once been a woman.

"How long—" he gasped, holding his neckerchief to his nose. "How long has this woman been dead?"

"Don't have a watch," said Mrs. Watson. "Maybe fifteen minutes. 'Bout when those screams died off."

Dr. Middleton stared, his blue eyes too wide. "This is—not possible. This progression of cellular decomposition--the clearly detectable presence of putrescine and cadaverine, the liquefaction of tissues—it's more…"

"She didn't look this bad when I rolled her up about ten minutes ago. Mind you, she was dead, all right. Just not *that* dead."

The doctor's stomach gave a kick, and he swallowed hard. Taking a step toward the bundle on the floor, he forced himself to examine the body, gesturing at Mrs. Watson to lift the lantern higher overhead. The shadows swung wildly around the room.

Whatever the cause, her abdomen had borne the brunt of it. Some violent outwrenching had blasted through the abdominal wall, but the doctor saw no telltale red lines or cuts from knife or scalpel, nor the peripheral punctures, tears, or defensive wounds one would associate with an animal attack.

It was as if the flesh itself had been eaten open from inside.

Not possible, he told himself. *Not possible*. He probed the wound, feeling the lipid globules of fatty tissue and the steaklike muscle, pushing aside the slippery and insistent folds of bowel. *Where in God's name is her uterus?* He felt chunks of tissue slide around his wrists. A fallopian tube rupture? A miscarriage? But where are the products of conception? Where is the baby?

Then something moved beneath his fingers. With an instinctive gasp, he drew his hand out of her.

It was covered with maggots.

Writhing, seething like a living glove, their segmented bodies contracting and lengthening, the maggots probed between his fingers, pushing forward with their quest, eyeless heads in search of putrefying flesh. Dr. Middleton scrabbled backwards, his heels digging for purchase as he scraped his hands over the filthy floor.

"I don't understand. I don't understand," he gasped. With a horrified, choking cough, he reached for the blanket and flung it over the body with its teeming hole.

Her hand jutted out, limp as a dead bird, and he noticed for the first time she was missing some fingers. The stumps had been ineptly wrapped, but he supposed it didn't matter now.

Mrs. Watson grasped the other end of the blanket and together, they rolled the corpse into a tight bundle. Now she was contained, it was better.

"We need to get her out," she said. The wind rose to a howl, shivering the canvas walls and rippling the roof. At the sound, their two heads raised simultaneously and fixed upon the entrance to the tent. Absurdly, the doctor recalled the scene from Macbeth, the red-handed king and queen startled by a knocking at the gate. *It will have blood*, he remembered, looking at Mrs. Watson. *Stones have been known to move and trees to speak, and all reveal the secret'st man of blood.*

Despite the gust, the odor from the body seemed to deepen and intensify. Even in the darkness, they could see the blanket had grown dark with the rank effluvium of the dead.

"Yes. She must be buried," the doctor murmured. "Immediately."

Mrs. Watson scoffed. "Don't have to tell me. Grady'll tend to it right enough. And Doc?"

"Yes?"

"I know I'm not the one paying your bills. And I suppose after tonight, you wouldn't never be passing out your coin for any services of mine."

The doctor thought, *This is entirely true.*

"But at the same time," she continued, "I have to know if you're a discreet fellow, one who can keep this to yourself. At least the details. Bad for trade, you understand. No need to have a plague of scandal. Or worse, a scandal of plague."

He nodded. "I can do so for a time, Mrs. Watson. If it be a plague, I fear I may not promise more than my duty permits." Realizing how stiff this sounded, he amended it. "I truly am sorry, you know."

"Fair enough." She nodded. "Buys me a few days, at least. I told Grady to say he dropped her at the depot, but if this is some catching sickness, I suppose that won't fly." Mrs. Watson drew a long sigh and said, "Very well. If anyone from the company inquires, as they might, all's you have to say is that the girl died before you got here. That's the plain truth, and it's about all you know anyway. 'Bout all I know myself."

As the wind rose again with an almost human keen, the woman turned to the forest, her forehead furrowed. "If the townsfolk ask," she said after a moment, "I suppose you can hand-wave it away. If someone presses you, just hem 'n haw awhile, and they'll chalk it up to a botched abortion." She let out a humorless chuckle.

"How did—" Dr. Middleton began. "How did it happen? This… circumstance? I'm afraid I did not inquire before."

"Everything was fine until the crying," replied Mrs. Watson with a shrug. "Right around sunset, she came in here all a-dither, telling me she heard a baby out there in the trees and she was worried about the poor mite. Even though the girls won't go far into those woods, she told me she was going in to fetch it if she could, supposing the child was abandoned."

"Why won't the girls go to the woods?" Dr. Middleton asked.

She waved a dismissive hand. "Bloodybones, spirits, and haunts, my mama would have said," but fell silent.

"And she was…attacked? By some animal?" The doctor remembered the woman's missing fingers, the makeshift bandage.

"I don't know. Two of my girls found her wandering by the forest's edge an hour or so later and brought her here. She came in babbling, not making a lick of sense. All she told me was, 'It was a baby, Mrs. Watson. A baby girl in a long white baptismal dress like the one my daughter wore.' When I asked her where the infant was, she gave this odd smile and whispered, 'Why, she's in me now.' Then she held up that hand, bleeding at the stumps with the fingers bitten off, and said, 'She was so pretty…and so hungry.'"

Dr. Middleton shivered, remembering Jude, his mouth full of knives.

"She fell to the ground then and laughed and laughed. I wrapped her hand and told her to rest, and so she did. About that time's when the gale started, and she fell into a fit. Wasn't in her right mind already, but this was worse. I dosed her up good with the laudanum, and we waited for you."

The doctor had withdrawn a small notebook from his inner pocket and was writing as she spoke. "What do you suppose was the cause of her bewilderment?"

She shook her head. "Most likely, I suppose she was bitten on the hand and ran from the animal off half-cocked, as one might. Perhaps she fell on something and knocked herself silly."

Dr. Middleton regarded her skeptically. "But the other—" He gestured helplessly. "The other symptoms? The vomitus of blood. The uncommonly rapid decay and dissolution of the flesh. How can those be from an attack by an animal?"

Her eyes met the doctor's. "I don't fuckin' know."

He stared at the bundle. From one end, a lock of light brown hair had slipped from the canvas and lay upon the floor. With an ache he could not name, the doctor reflected that this very morning, the woman had probably brushed it and put it in a braid. She had gone about her business, smiled at her friends, had seen the sun shed dappled gold between the pines and loved it as a beautiful thing.

"What was her name?" he asked. "This good lady?"

Mrs. Watson's eyebrows rose, and she gave him another appraising look. It was not so cold this time. Not at all.

"Her name was Clara," she answered, and looked away.

Outside, the wind from the forest grew louder.

After some time, Grady came back into the tent. He'd traveled down the dark road to Juniper to fetch the wheelbarrow from Hodges' Mercantile, knowing he would surely need it if any burying was to be done before morning. *Can't carry her over my shoulder*, he'd mused. *She wouldn't hold together but a minute.*

All down the road to town, the wind had pushed at him, stabbing inside seams and through his wet hair, and finally, in the silver light from the cold and vacant moon, he found his defenses and distractions fall away until there was only the dark and the wood and the truth.

The voices, he realized, tightening his coat. *The whispers. And the stench. It's a blood gale and you know it. Can't be nothing else. It's awake. The woods are hungry.*

At first, he'd supposed the reek had come from Clara, from the black spatter she'd spasmed from her mouth into his, fouling his clothes and his hair. But he'd changed the shirt and washed himself outside while Mrs. Watson talked to the doc, rubbing his head as clean as it ever got. Yet still the wind carried the red scent, coppery and rank, heavy with flesh and rot.

The woods are hungry.

Grady hurried faster, hand clutched around the old poppet, muttering the ancient charm over and over until the words made no sense in his mind or his mouth anymore, carefully pressing himself to the side of the embankment farthest from the grasping junipers that gave the town its name, the trees with their old roots tangled in the hard and selfish earth.

Dug too deep. Woke something up. He shivered, and when a tree scratched his coat with its questing fingers, Grady shrieked like a catamount and ran the rest of the way into town. By the time he came back, the wheelbarrow all a-rattle, the encampment filled him with a relief so profound he nearly wept.

When he came inside, he saw only Mrs. Watson in her customary place on the corner stool, her elbows braced against her knees in an attitude of weariness he felt himself.

"You got what you needed in town?" she asked when he came in. "Took you long enough."

He nodded. "I did, ma'am. Found a wheelbarrow at Hodges', as I said, and brung it straightaway. Soon as I see the doc over to his boardinghouse, I'll come back and start on the grave for poor Clara. Best be done before the morning."

Mrs. Watson drew on her cigarette, leaning back against the wood support. "Well, you won't have to worry. Doc's on his way already. Saved you a trip out n' back."

Grady's eyes grew wide. "But that ain't possible."

"Why the hell not?"

"I ain't seen him on the road. Neither coming nor going. So where the hell'd he go?"

Mrs. Watson frowned. "I pointed him the way. Offered to walk with him myself, but he turned it down. Declared he'd probably take the forest cutoff, and I guess he might. Moon's full out, so it's light enough. There's no other way besides the road, and that's a longer trek." She shrugged and licked her fingers, pinching off the butt-end of her cigarette. "Who knows? He mighta passed you while you were at the mercantile. I notice the wind's finally died down, so there's that, at least."

Grady nodded. "Yes, ma'am. There is that."

Letter, September 29, 1904, from Dr. Alfred Middleton to Mr. Frank Poole:

POST SCRIPTUM

My dear Frank, it is well past midnight in the encampment, and I have at last concluded my business here. Mr. Grady returns momentarily from the town, and from there, poor Clara will be taken for burial.

As for me, I feel ready for burial myself. I am quite fatigued. On the morrow, I shall return and begin an investigation of a more considered nature into the etiology of this woman's strange condition, particularly to determine if the disease be communicable to others, and if so, by what means.

But not tonight. Good God, not tonight.

If one is to believe the maps of this territory, the town is not far, perhaps a mile. Mrs. Watson has directed me to the road, but according to my map, there is an even shorter route by the forest path, if I interpret it correctly. Though overgrown, it is clearly the more direct way. I thought to wait for Mr. Grady's return, but now I believe I shall venture forward now without further inconveniencing the man.

My medical bag is packed away, and I have righted the objects here and rewrapped the body. From the uncertain liquid sound when I wrapped the blanketed remains in a length of army duck, there is little left to see that resembles a woman.

We are meat, Frank. We are only meat, and 'he that soweth to his own flesh will from the flesh reap corruption.' Is it not so?

The wind howls through the juniper pines, and it seems I too can hear a kind of crying from within the woods, as I did on my approach. I find myself thinking of Jude when he was just a child, and he would weep like that.

How odd.

Surely the story Clara told of a babe in the woods was mere delusion, some apoplectic vision, perhaps, or a hallucination caused by her disorientation and loss of limbs. As for me, I need fear no "bloodybones and ha'ants,' as Mrs. Watson's mother would put it. No. To assume otherwise would be absurd, and above all, I am a man of science. No pagan tokens for me, thank you.

As it is late, I do believe I shall make my way to Juniper at once. Tomorrow morning, I shall write to you before a pleasant fire in the boarding-house with my feet on the hearth. Until then, I suppose I'll "shiver the whole night through," as the song says.

Best regards, my dear friend Frank,

A. Middleton

When the dawn came, Grady stared out of the tent-flap, running his thumb over the little homemade poppet and considering the wind. It blew from the east now, from the valley and not from the forest, a tame and gentle breeze to cool the morning. It smelled of earth and sun, and pine, and not a hint of blood.

Back asleep at last, he thought, and then, *But for how long?*

Some hours before, when Clara's body was awkwardly stowed in the wheelbarrow, Mrs. Watson had given Grady a stern admonition to keep an eye out for the doctor, just in case. Grady had nodded obliging-ly, knowing he'd never see the man again. Not if the doc had ventured into the woods. Not when the ill wind was blowing like it was.

Mrs. Watson asked, "Ain't you afraid of the forest like the rest?"

"No more'n usual, ma'am," Grady answered, lifting the wheelbar-row. With that, he made for the trees.

He knew the place. His father had showed him, as his father's father had, and his father too. The clearing in the woods. The circle of ancient, stunted pines, their limbs stretched out like grasping fingers.

The ancient grey stone for the Old Ones stained red with steam-ing blood.

It's your place, he said to them silently as he passed beneath the trees, *but I ain't coming here empty-handed.*

With a resolute look, Grady lowered the wheelbarrow and picked up his shovel.

There was digging to be done.

Shadows
Marie Casey

In the simplest of terms, shadows are defined as the absence of light due to the obstruction of something which light cannot pierce through. They exist because they cannot be graced with light. Logically sound, but logic does not equate to morality. To take away the light is as cruel as taking away a life out of boredom. Lights out, bye-bye. And there is nothing more cruel than a bored human.

In terms of Brattlebury, humans were stacked and collected and given nothing to do. They wandered hallways and stared at walls for countless hours. You could say, all they managed to do was cast shadows. Their existence was collective as opposed to individualized. Cattled from one room to another. Much of the staff could only see black and white; you were a patient or you were not. Insane or just fine. One of them or not. The human brain works like that naturally. Compartments help make sense of the world.

However, the logic of Brattlebury was that the sickness that burdened these women should be locked away. Fill them up with mind-altering medication and insist on change. The insistence upon change worked, but not in the fashion the doctors had hoped. Out of frustration, they got creative and casted far more shadows than any patient had done on their own. The darkness lingered in the walls of Brattlebury and some swore the shadows had a will of their own. These were all things Sylvia Rose had yet to learn.

Sylvia jittered and her teeth chattered. Violent vibrations stiffed her joints and she walked rigidly. Sylvia grew up respecting her parents and teachers. *Yes, sir* and *yes, ma'am* flowed easily from her lips. She was never rude, not now and not then. And as she followed Nurse Gertrude under a fluorescent sky and Nurse Gertrude spouted out her list of Brattlebury rules, Sylvia nodded agreeably.

"No food outside the cafeteria. No going to other people's rooms without explicit permission from a staff member. All medication is to be taken at the nurses' station and under no circumstances are you to disobey direct orders from staff..." She continued for several minutes. It was an extensive list of rules which Nurse Gertrude recited countless times before. Rules helped everyone get along and she was a strong enforcer of them. She had a modified one for returning patients, but that was a rare occasion. Not many people left and those who did, vanished without a trace.

Sylvia nodded with a smile, trying to mask the shake in her hands and glisten on her forehead. The hum of groans and cries from other patients was always a surprise to new guests. The patients either shuffled without eye contact or stared intently in their direction. The patients showed a particular interest in Sylvia. New meat and naive to boot. It was written all over her face; this place was not meant for a woman of such innocent grace and time was running out for it to remain.

They entered a patient room and Nurse Gertrude took the suitcase out of Sylvia's hands and placed it on the bed. She proceeded to open and shuffle through what it contained. Various articles of clothing, a comb, and a copy of As I Lay Dying by William Faulkner. Nurse Gertrude inspected the book with a critical eye, flipping through the pages and insisting something would drop out. Patients were resourceful in their deceit and would hide the most insidious objects such as razor blades in the most harmless of places. A hauntingly comparable analogy to Brattlebury itself. However, nothing did drop out, it was simply a book that Sylvia's English teacher encouraged her to read. Sylvia had run into Mrs. Williams at the grocery store three weeks ago holding the multiple bottles of aspirin that would trigger the series of events that would lead her to Brattlebury. She told me all this, her story. Heartbreaking and lonely girl.

Nurse Gertrude put away her suspicious eyes and dropped her demeanor to a more welcoming one. Sylvia stood with her hands flexed up and her body swaying back and forth. No doubt a nervous tick depicting her truly harmless disposition.

A woman little older than Sylvia walked into the room with a gilded disdain. She twirled around Sylvia and caused notable tension to form in Sylvia's upper back.

"Fresh," she giggled.

"Zoey, you be nice," Nurse Gertrude growled. "I expect you to show her to the cafeteria in thirty minutes, do you understand me?"

"Yes, sir," she grinned and gave an exaggerated salute.

Nurse Gertrude rolled her eyes and exited the room.

Sylvia went to salvage her belongings that were now spread across the cot. A Brattlebury welcome. Zoey watched with the same grin and Sylvia tried to ignore her but kept looking up to meet her glaring eyes. Sylvia took multiple deep breaths as if she could not swallow enough air. The air in Brattlebury was different, heavier than normal. Most struggled to adjust. Only shallow breaths were welcomed.

"What did you mean by *fresh*?" Sylvia asked.

"You've never been to a place like this before or even left the comfort of your suburban home, I can tell. You can always tell, but especially with you."

"How?"

"It's the way you look, your eyes. Eyes always change once they have been in a place like this."

⁂

They walked together to the cafeteria in silence. Organized chaos filled the room. With chatter and barking, the energy flowed wild. Unkempt hair and poor table manners illuminated the room, though everyone sat in their chairs. It was likely due to the watchful eyes from each corner of the room. They scanned over the crowd and everyone knew their place.

With trays of discolored mash potatoes and cardboard-textured meatloaf, they sat down with their questionable food at a table. Three other women looked up at them in greeting. One with glasses and curly hair. One older than the rest with gray hair. One so skinny and frail, Sylvia looked strong in comparison.

"Who's the new girl?" the one with curls bellowed.

"I'm Sylvia." She extended out her hand but was denied a shake. She retreated and fog covered her face.

"Dita." The older woman held out her hand.

Sylvia's head lifted slightly and reached out.

"This is Rosalie," Dita pointed to the frail one, "and this is Susan."

Susan rolled her eyes at the situation and poked at her glop of mashed potatoes.

"First time, huh?"

Sylvia nodded, avoiding eye contact.

"Figured. Your skin is still full of color and there is still light in your eyes. All that light will make it hard to see the dark spots that will help you survive in this place."

Sylvia looked to her roommate, Zoey, who was mid-bite of her meatloaf, for interpretation. She chewed and mumbled with food in her mouth, "I don't know what she's talking about, either. You just look like you left high school music class, is all. Plus, let's face it, all new people here are new here."

Sylvia did not understand it at the time but her naivete would soon come to an end.

"Listen, this place will make you crazy if you don't have a few good people to talk to."

Everyone somberly nodded in agreement.

"What are you in for? Did you murder your husband or something?" Susan asked.

Spit got caught in Sylvia's throat and she choked. "No, I am not married and if I was, I would never."

Susan, Rosalie, and Zoey gave each other side eyes before bursting with laughter. Dita gave a gentle slap on Susan's shoulder.

"Girls, leave her alone. Y'all are a bunch of heartless monsters. Stop pretending like you don't remember what your first few days here were like," Dita snarled at the other three women. She grabbed Sylvia's hand from across the table. "They are just giving you a hard time because they got nothing better to do. You tell your story when and if you want to, ya hear? That's the only power we got in this place."

Sylvia nodded.

"People don't come here crazy but they will stay here crazy, remember that." She gave a firm squeeze to Sylvia's hand and went back to spooning her mash potatoes. Sylvia followed suit, mirroring what the others did.

"Oh, look who is walking among the living." Rosalie pointed at a pale faced woman with blackened eyes. She shuffled in hospital slippers with ease, but her fists were clenched. The room went quiet watching her. Polly Griswold was no different than Sylvia a few months ago. Unsure and frightened but now a woman who brought significant discomfort to a crowd and deemed too insane for listening ear. A woman who screamed in tones that haunted even the staff's dreams. She went on and on about the secrets of Brattlebury. Louder and louder she made her voice, but no one wanted to acknowledge. I did, of course, but that also was one reason people believed she suffered from insanity.

"Who is that?"

"Polly, she's the prime example of what this place can do to you," Dita said.

Zoey giggled. "She talks to shadow people and about people going missing. She has lost her damn mind and she hasn't even been here that long."

"Shadow people?"

"She went crazy being here. It happens, just try to avoid her."

A group of young medical residents waited for Dr. Walters in the front lobby of Brattlebury. Eager, but sitting with respectful acquiescence. It was the beginning of their psychiatric rotation. The old batch was out, and these new young men would be put up to a true test of their medical knowledge. Working in madness always had its challenges.

"Do you think we will get to meet the women today?" Colin whispered.

"Hungry to meet your new girlfriend? You dog you," Paul snorted.

"Dr. Walters will see you now," a nurse announced.

The group of medical residents stood up and followed the nurse into the hospital hallways.

Colin slapped Paul's shoulder. "I didn't mean it like that."

"Sure thing, bud," the sarcasm echoed.

Colin rubbed his forehead in embarrassment. I always like to think Colin meant well. But, even the most open-minded medical residents that embellished the hallways of Brattlebury struggled to understand the patients properly. *These women were unwell*, they would hear over and over again. A broad term with little fact surrounding it. When a heart is unwell, there are several notable facts to write down. A leaky valve, muscle deterioration, or a blocked artery. What was wrong could be known, but this was not so clear with the mentally insane.

What there was to know about insanity was that it described the inability to fit in with society in some way. A textbook-type definition that explained little and gave no justifications for their given treatments. Treatment driven by opinion. There wasn't anything any of these medical professionals found that was notably wrong with the mass majority, only nonconformity. And yet, thousands of women filtered in and out of this place deemed unwell.

One by one, the medical residents filled the office of the prominent psychiatric doctor. It was not big enough for all of them to comfortably sit, as there were only two spare chairs. A few knelt on the floor and others leaned up against the walls.

"Afternoon, gentlemen," Dr. Walters greeted. He continued spewing out biographical details about himself, including the note that he once attended the same medical school as the young men. He regaled them with his time overseas and a few hospital war stories, presenting himself as a man who lived a life with many climatic moments. His eyes bore the burden of many endings, yet he appeared to be a man who could talk excessively about himself with significant joy on his face.

"How did you end up here at Brattlebury?" asked one of the individuals fortunate enough to find a chair.

"I wanted to work more with women. I spent so much time in the war working with men, that I grew bored. I needed a challenge. In recent years, there has been an epidemic of hysteria. The women of this country need help more than ever, and there I found a need for my expertise. An opportunity if you will." He nodded profusely as if he was trying to convince himself, as well as the young men.

"Do you have an explanation or theory on how working with

women is different from men?"

"Yes, I do. With women, there is a lot of shame. It overwhelms them and controls many of their decisions and actions. They become so overwhelmed with this unreasonable feeling and struggle to gain a deeper understanding. Men have shame for specific short-term things, but women carry shame as a constant. Their inferiority to male accomplishments gets lodged in their brain, driving many hysterical. It is a hard problem to crack." Dr. Walters massaged his hands together, pursing his lips.

Colin audibly gulped. His eyes wandered the room to monitor the reactions of his fellow classmates. There was a clear consensus of acceptance.

"Have you been able to crack them?" an accepting young man asked.

Dr. Walters let out a gasp of laughter. "No, my boy. I am not sure it will be a mystery that men of our era will ever fully understand. However, I have been conducting a variety of experimental treatments that have proven to have some effective therapeutic qualities. I hope to establish great advancements of understanding in my lifetime."

"Can you go into more detail about these experimental treatments?"

"It's hard to explain in the time we have, but essentially, I am trying to retrain their perceptions by manipulating the electromagnetic spectrum. They need to perceive themselves as we do." His shortness could not have been a mistake. It was a calculated manipulation of the young medical residents. Dr. Walters's ego would not allow him to keep his mouth fully shut about his experiments, but the experiments would surely be shut down if all the details were exposed.

Silence pierced through.

Colin took a deep breath and tried to swallow the heavy Brattlebury air. The air affected even the privileged here. "In what ways do these women carry their shame? As in, how do they typically behave?"

"Women are here for all kinds of strange behaviors. We have some here for their own safety, of course. Some display self-harming behaviors and their husbands express concern that they are a danger to themselves. Others are rather sexually active, and some have even more bizarre behaviors we could talk about all day."

Paul nudged Colin and let out a subtle giggle which sounded like a fast exhale. Blood rushed to Colin's cheeks.

"They are not typical behaviors we like to see from women," the doctor ended.

"How would you go about treating that?" Colin dug further.

"Innovation."

In a gray studded chair, a stocky man with glasses and a large belly sat across from Sylvia. She wiggled her rear and dug her fingernails into the fabric of a couch that smelled of somber body odor and sweat.

After withstanding the general discomfort of Brattlebury and the endless intrusive questioning, drowning felt both impossible and probable. Sylvia leaned into the warm breeze that leaked from the cracked window and in a strong gust, she would later tell me, she made a wish. A wish for the wind to grow powerful enough to shatter the glass and impale her face.

"It says here that you told the doctor at the hospital that you felt lost, that the reason you did what you did was because you felt lost. Can you explain to me what you mean by that?" He tapped the end of his pen on his notepad.

Sylvia shrugged. It's not an easy feeling to convey. There never appears to be a correct order of words to articulate such a feeling. It's like that moment when you lose your mother at the grocery store. Deep down you know she must be in another aisle but still, the shelves grow taller, and the products become alien. Strangers get stranger and light becomes blinding. The world spins and time speeds up. Panic sets in and hope vanishes in the wind. None of it makes sense, but you can feel it, and feelings don't have to make sense. However, in Sylvia's case, there was no mother and there was no grocery store. Just a perpetual forlorn feeling trapped inside her amygdala. It was unreasonable but yet, it was there. It was always there.

"Do you remember saying that?" he pushed further.

"Not really," she lied. "I don't remember much from the hospital." She did remember and when she tried to describe the feeling to the doctor, he ended up placing her at Brattlebury.

Dr. Walters nodded and scribbled a series of notes which made radical speculations of both her temperament and her ability to reason. He had swiped this patient to be his own, even though she was set to be taken on by a new medical resident the following day. It was not her story or what she had done to herself a few weeks prior that interested him. Sylvia met a specific criterion for the doctor, she had no one waiting for her on the other side.

"Okay, okay. What about the events leading up to being in the hospital? Do you know what you did to yourself?"

Sylvia nodded and her eyes began to swell. Tears dripped and dropped from her cheek. Her hands trembled as her mind traveled. "Do you think God will ever forgive me?"

The doctor gave a deep sigh. He was not a good candidate for such a question, nevertheless, it was a question he was often asked. "This is not for me to decide, my dear." He leaned forward and placed his hand on her knee. "However, I do want to help you get better. Will you let me help you?"

Sylvia gripped onto his hand with desperation and whimpered a melody of sorrow. She cried yes and gave an effort to smile at him. It was enough to seal the deal.

"Tomorrow we will begin."

The hallway echoed with the sound of Sylvia's passing. Despite her efforts to walk without being noticed, wandering eyes followed her as she walked back to her room. From patients to staff, everyone saw her, and everyone was curious. The attention roasted her skin and she walked rawly down the hall.

As she turned the corner, she came face to face with the infamous Polly. With spine shakes and shifty eyes, Sylvia kept her head down. Despite her blatant avoidance, Polly went out of her way to make her presence known. Step by step. Shift by shift.

"It's not true what they say about me you know. Well, some of it is," she laughed. "I saw you left Doctor Walters office and I hope you soon won't understand. Did he offer you a special treatment?"

"I don't know," Sylvia whispered.

"The shadows aren't the problem, it's the treatments. Promise me you won't do it."

Sylvia tried to escape with dodging footwork, but Polly kept up with her footing. She grabbed Sylvia's arm and panic jolted throughout Sylvia's body.

"Don't do the treatments, do you understand me? And if you do, do not fear the shadows. Dr. Walters is malevolent. He's the crazy one here." Her voice grew louder and louder and her grip got tighter and tighter. Her screeches caught the attention of an orderly.

"Polly, hands off!"

"Don't do it!" she continued to scream as the orderly dragged her away.

⚜

Sylvia took a seat on a padded chair. She stared intently at the restraints attached to the arms of the chair and then the foreign machinery placed in front of her. However, she smiled as Dr. Walters entered the room. Armed in a white coat and notebook in hand, he made no effort at acknowledging her presence. He entered the room focused on the task in mind. He made a few adjustments to dials and took a seat adjacent to her.

"Afternoon, Sylvia."

"Afternoon, Doctor. Can I ask you something?

"Sure."

"Is this the same treatment Polly gets?"

Only after she said, *Polly,* did the doctor make the effort to connect eyes. Boldness in his patients was not a favorable trait for Dr. Walters.

"Why do you ask?"

"She told me not to agree to it, but everyone says she is crazy." Everyone did say she was crazy. After her encounter, Nurse Gertrude came by her room to check for injury. Even she told Sylvia not to give much thought to Polly, that she was *unwell.* There were so many voices in Brattlebury in such a short amount of time, it was a task for Sylvia to know who to trust.

"Ah, I see. Polly is an unusual and stubborn woman. Despite my efforts, she continues to linger without my guidance. However, it's not appropriate for me to talk about someone else's treatment. So, we are going to focus on you and getting you well, okay?"

Sylvia agreed. They went over a medical history which did not entail much more than a clean break and healing of her ulna when she was seven. She had disobeyed her father's request not to run while with her hands full and fell on a curb in the perfect way that cracked the bone and tarnished her confidence. Otherwise, Sylvia was a physically healthy individual.

Sitting back, the chair reclined, Sylvia allowed for her wrists to be strapped down. Dr. Walters explained it was to ensure she stayed still, as the flashing lights can be startling. She squirmed as the fabric itched her wrists, but she remained compliant and kept her mouth shut as the doctor worked. He was focusing deeply on dials and mechanical doo-hickeys. He appeared more focused on his calculations with Sylvia than he was with Polly. Polly was a failure in his eyes, but she was a success in mine. She can now see the dark spots with great ease.

Dr. Walters told Sylvia to relax and prepare for a series of flashing lights. The machine clicked and clanged. A lens moved to the front of her face, inches from her eyes.

"Nothing to be afraid of, my dear. It's only noise," Dr. Walters explained, but sweat formed on her brow. There was nothing like being told how to feel when loud machinery screamed in your face, but that was Dr. Walters for you. Tell patients what to do and expect no freewill. Sylvia jolted backwards at the second flash. Blinding lights made it difficult to watch. Nevertheless, with the progression of lights flashing in her eyes, came the smell of burnt hair and flesh. An unsightly scene I wished I did not see.

Sylvia did not scream and eventually stopped wiggling. She stared directly into the lens and did not move. Her mouth fell open and emotion disappeared from her face. There was no more fear, as the doctor had ordered.

As the flashes continued, the doctor watched closely and took notes.

Colin opened the office window and was greeted by a gust of spring air. He sat in a bare room, consisting of two chairs, a desk, and the briefcase he brought in. Tapping his pen, he had little to do on his second day of rotation. He waited impatiently to meet his second patient of the day.

There was a significant jitter in his step this morning before his first patient. During his arrival a couple hours ago, he was greeted by a woman screaming at the walls. She did appear to be with anyone and had gotten so upset that an orderly had to pin her down to the ground to calm her. There were panic gasps as he waited for his first patient to be her, but it was not the same woman. She was dismissive to his questions but did not scream. Their session came and went.

He peeked out of his office to find the nurses station vacant. Being ten minutes past the appointment time, he ventured out into the hallway and was confronted by muffled whispers in the distance. He found Nurse Gertrude and an orderly across the hall behind a cracked door. They made eye contact and Colin threw up his hands in an edgy impatience.

"What's going on?" he asked.

Nurse Gertrude took a moment to breathe. "We cannot seem to find your next patient, Sylvia. She has been missing since this morning. I just had an orderly check. She was around for a bed check last night but has seemingly vanished in the night." Her throat constricted and her voice cracked.

Nurse Gertrude was one of the few staff members that the patients liked. She was the one to go to when a patient needed things and the one to talk to when things got tough with another patient. She was a healer and a problem solver through and through, but when it came to confronting doctors, her voice buckled.

"What is the protocol for a missing patient?"

"Well, we have searched the grounds and we are searching again. Then if we still cannot find her, we will contact the local authorities to keep an eye out for her. I don't understand how she could have left the building. Her room and ward would have been locked." Sweat was forming around her brow. She wiped it from her forehead as the young resident looked away. She knew of the many mysteries of Brattlebury but, she did not talk about it. Unexplainable phenomena happened here and for as much as she tried to deny the cries of many of the patients at Brattlebury, I like to think she knew some were not as crazy as they sounded. If anyone was to listen, it would be Nurse Gertrude.

With rolling eyes, Colin turned around and walked back to his empty office. Irritation boiled from his skin. Nurse Gertrude shuffled after him, but the shape of his shoulder hunch gave indication of his current mindset. As he entered his office, he slammed the door shut.

She left Colin to the privacy of his office. Nurse Gertrude was no stranger to the hallways of Brattlebury and she walked with determination in her stride. She appeared more bothered by this disappearance than any other before. I am not sure why exactly, but Sylvia had barely made a dent in her bed before vanishing. That had to have bothered Nurse Gertrude.

She entered the Ward C nurses station and opened a filing cabinet. Inside was a clipboard holding a crucial piece of information. The bed check role call for Sylvia was signed off, but who signed off on it made her drop the clipboard on the floor. Dr. Walters. A doctor doing a bed check was unheard of and only one person in this place screamed of such insanity.

She left the nurses station and hustled down another hallway. Grabbing her keys, she looked both ways in the hallway before opening this particular patient's door. She opened to find the patient lying on the floor. The patient did not lift their head or make any indication that someone had entered the room. She breathed slowly as the orderly from this morning had crushed her rib cage.

"Polly?"

⚜

Overnight shifts brought a stillness to Brattlebury. All the patients were asleep and there was little excitement to listen for. However, it was long and unsettling. The sounds did not cease but changed, and boredom brought on untamed thoughts. After losing Sylvia a few days back, Nurse Gertrude had switched with another nurse to assess how she could have escaped. The hospital reported her missing, then went silent over the ordeal. It was like she never existed.

She checked the locks, she walked the halls, she triple-checked each step. There were many things to say about Brattlebury, but the nighttime security was sound. There was nowhere for a patient to go without the aid of a staff member.

She sat at the nurse's station with a pile of completed paperwork stacked in front of her. The fluorescent lights in the room flickered and buzzed. It was a typical occurrence, as the lights were old, and the building was even older. The whistle of another nurse walking by came and went. They waved at each other as she passed, and Nurse Gertrude gazed upon the shadow that followed her.

When she had gone to visit Polly, she would not speak to Nurse Gertrude. She ignored all her questions and queries. She did not move and barely breathed. She was beaten and broken at that time. However, once Nurse Gertrude said Sylvia's name, she responded, *Look for the shadows.*

As the shadow of her fellow nurse disappeared, Nurse Gertrude's eyes shifted a few feet away at another shadow trailing behind. No person appeared to be in the hallway nor any moving objects. Nothing could be the cause of the human-shaped shadow on the wall that moved down the hall. Nothing known to people outside of Brattlebury, at least.

She gasped and jolted backwards in her chair. The shadow stopped moving as if it was startled by Nurse Gertrude's movements. She stared at the shadow before it moved again.

Look for the shadows.

She stood to follow the shadow down the hall. It moved slowly and deliberately, as did Nurse Gertrude. It stopped in front of a room and slipped through the crack of the door. Her hand shook as adrenaline pumped throughout her body. Fumbling her keys, she crept up to the familiar door.

"Polly?" She flicked on the lights to find Polly sitting upright on her bed staring at the wall in front of her. On it were a number of human shaped shadows. "Polly?" she said once more.

Polly giggled and clapped. "You followed the shadows!" she howled and swung her feet into the air. Her giddiness lightened the energy in the room, but the confusion remained.

Nurse Gertrude inched herself away from the shadows and towards Polly. She took a hesitant seat on the edge of the bed and stared at the shadows. Four shadows and myself. We all look the same. Outline of a body, with the absence of light. However, despite all our similarities, she focused on one in particular. The shadow with its hands flexed up and the body that swayed back and forth.

With realization, she broke her gaze to look at Polly, who sat with tears in her eyes and a smile on her face. Her own eyes began to well up and she asked, "Sylvia?"

Polly nodded yes, and we told her our story.

The Leeches will Lead Us

Jeremy Megargee

His unwashed hands twist deeper into the wound, knuckles bullying past soft organs and inflamed tissue. Resistance makes sweat pour from his brow into that ragged crimson aperture, fluid mixing with fluid. His pupils are little black pinpricks, neurotic weasel eyes, and he nibbles into his drooping lip as he curls his wrist past that naughty wet colon worm and takes a firm grip of the spleen into his balled fist. He calls for an artificial leech, and a sweaty assistant places the metallic cylinder into his free hand. Carron plunges the tube into the opening of the torso, a few errant rust flakes breaking from the exterior, and he uses the rotating blades to glide across the spleen, sucking up the bad blood with the attached tube. The patient gurgles on the table, laudanum barely holding the anguish at bay, and Carron hushes him by twisting up a rag and forcing those quivering jaws to bite down on it.

The operating theater is brimming with ticketed spectators, dozens of gore-starved faces staring down at the butchery from circular rafters. They guffaw and leer and stuff peanuts into their drooling maws, tossing the shells down to the filthy floor at Carron's feet. Opportunistic rodents dart out from shadowed crannies and make quick work of the shells, munching as the surgeon pulls his fingers from that red slit and shakes them, letting the blood droplets fly, splattering the lips and noses of the spectators in the front row. They react with glee, akin to children getting splashed by baby seals on some leisure beach in the South Pacific.

The surgeon turns to his assistant and he wipes at his apron, smearing scarlet stains across it, creating patterns that resemble ruined red flowers in a garden that is best left to the damned. "I've bled him as well as he can be bled. Hope for pus, lest the rot take hold. It's out of our control now."

Carron sighs, patting his assistant's cheek, leaving little blood-speckled fingerprints on the flesh. The boy is frail, just an urchin, and the surgeon has sincere doubts that he'll do what is being asked of him. But Carron does not care. His thoughts are elsewhere, and soon his body will follow them. "Stitch him up and sit with him. Brandy if he can stand it, but if you see it bubbling up from the wound, discontinue and administer no more."

He turns and clamps one nostril to blow a wad of snot out onto the floor, the flensing knives and chipped scalpels jangling from the belt wrapped around his waist. Then Carron lifts his head to the men and women crowded like sardines in the rafters, allowing his voice to boom and carry, making a performance of it. "The wonders of modern medicine, ladies and gentlemen. This poor wretch comes complaining of a gut-ache, and it's found that the blood circulation around his spleen has gone sour. Being that it's midwinter and the leeches are hard to breed, we utilized this fine contraption, a better tool than its living brethren, and if God is merciful, his insides will close without infection, and he'll have a few more years with his children."

There are a handful of medical students in attendance that take notes, but the vast majority of the hoople-heads just gape, not under-

JEREMY MEGARGEE

standing the procedure at all, but having craved a bit of nastiness on the chill February evening before they scurried off in search of liquor and prostitutes.

"The nurses will be passing the collection plate to donate, if you're able, for science does come at a cost. And remember, the University is still seeking fresh cadavers and will pay handsomely but be warned--do not bring them weeks cold bodies from the grave or you'll leave, not with coin, but with the constable's manacles on your wrists. Our research cadavers must be lukewarm, the breath of life just a few days departed, and the fee will be doubled for intact brains that have not yet begun to putrefy."

The surgeon feels that familiar weariness settle into his soul. It's like he's speaking to bodies that lack spirits, and perhaps it's the profession that has instilled it in him, a lack of empathy and humanity when conversing with his fellow man. Every pair of eyes he meets in the operating theater views him with callous disregard, seeing him not as a healer, but a torturer.

There are moments like this, after a surgery has concluded, when he's tempted to leap up into the mass of them and start cutting and gouging, flaying the damned tender skinbags raw in search of something meaningful, even if it is the most rudimentary spark of intelligence or imagination.

He knows it's useless to let such ruminations swirl in his head. He'll only frustrate himself, so he offers a parting smile to the audience, putting as much fabricated benevolence into it as he can. He strides through the tattered sheets exiting the theater, and soon his feet are pounding cobblestones, his top hat affixed to his head and his wool overcoat swirling in the night breeze.

It cannot all be folly. There is still his sacred project, something so near and dear to his heart that just thinking about it sends a flood of serotonin into his exhausted system. It'll scratch him out a place in history, and his colleagues will boil in their jealousy when they see his dreams come to fruition. The secret of the leech, the power of the leech, all of it hinging on those sleek black parasites...

He grins to himself in the bitter dark, his handlebar moustache twitching on his upper lip, a content caterpillar crawling its way to fame and fortune. He won't be a two-bit sawbones on Saccharine Street forever. Hubert Carron is built for more.

But for now, it's time for a dollop of well-earned leisure. Something to sap the cold from his bones and string together a song in his heart. Even the good doctor needs his medicine.

The opium den is a dark little cave filled with tasseled pillows and ornate curtains of deep scarlet, and Carron luxuriates in the gloom, manipulating the long pipe over the oil lamp and breathing deeply of the vapors that twirl out. He lounges back, eyelids fluttering, his head becoming a dreamy place where thoughts glop up together in one big colorful mess of saltwater taffy. He silently praises the poppy, and he suckles loyally at the teats of Mother Nature for the gift of this stress-dissolving bliss.

He had hoped to indulge in his vice alone, but Professor Moldovian finds him there and nestles close to him in the shadows, seeing an opportunity for two academics to cluck at each other like egocentric hens. Carron can barely see the man amidst the smoke and the fluttering light of the oil lamps, his face just a tiny quivering moon in the blackness, but heat bakes from Moldovian's body, and it's enough to irritate the surgeon. Carron wishes he'd get up and scurry off to his extracurricular affairs. The good professor is known to lap at brothel twat after he's had his opium, but he seems intent to linger this time around, and he's in the mood to provoke.

"This obsession with those slimy worms, Hubert. What can be

gleaned from them? They're becoming archaic. I'd warrant ten years from now, they'll have no place in medicine at all."

Carron scoffs, and if side-eyeing could kill a man, Moldovian would drop dead right there on the burnt carpet.

"You underestimate the leech, Professor. They are remarkable specimens. A living hermaphrodite that sups on blood, and can you imagine a more perfect parasite? I've often proposed they develop a relationship with the host they're feeding from. Something symbiotic. And if that level of awareness exists in the leech, couldn't some form of sentience be reached, even in the confines of dead tissue?"

"Preposterous. I can think of no animal lower on the totem pole. Praise the great elephants of the Orient, or even the apes, but I'll give no deep scientific thought to those little blood-crazed gluttons."

The professor chuckles before taking another inhalation from his pipe, and Carron sees a yellowing in the whites of his eyes. Jaundice. He sincerely hopes the man's liver quits on him soon so that he can take his criticisms into a shallow grave.

"There are rumors that you've been hoarding the live ones, old boy. Doctors claim there's a shortage in this borough, and they've been forced into using the man-made equivalent. I dare say those infernal instruments are more humane. I'll take an artificial leech over a squiggling river worm if I ever find myself on your slab."

He slaps Carron on the back, and the grimace on the surgeon's face only deepens. The opium isn't having its usual calming effect thanks to the naysayer and his babbling mouth.

"Take care with that loose talk. A rumor is a dangerous thing. Sometimes it grows teeth, and it might be prone to bite…" Carron glares at that oval of moon-face, and there's terrible hardness in his eyes. His gaze reflects light from the oil lamps, and it has an almost daemonic effect. It doesn't take long for Moldovian to wither, as all cowardly blowhards do when confronted directly, and his simpering overtakes his contrarian mood.

"I meant no offense, Hubert. You know I have a deep admiration for your work. I merely jest, which I blame on imbibing a bit too much tonight. These foreign devils and their poppies making foes of old friends! I'll not have it. I'm of a mind to find myself a warm bed and a warmer woman to share it with..."

"A fine idea, professor. And if you ever do find yourself on my *slab*--as you so eloquently put it--rest assured you'll receive the most attentive care that I'm capable of administering to you."

Carron's lips split open, and a grin of crooked tombstone teeth shows itself in the haze of smoke. The surgeon leans back into the inky dark until nothing but the grin is shining, and Moldovian is quick to gather up his cape and scarf. He offers a curt nod and his own little half-hearted smile in return, and then he's off down the twisting fabric corridors, bound for a hasty exit.

The surgeon remains, and he's grateful for the silent time. He cranes his neck back and blows dragon breath overhead, watching the tendrils curl up into amorphous patterns. The longer he looks into the smoke, the more he sees slithering forms twisting and twining together. A bulbous ball of obsidian-bodies, lords and ladies of the leech breed, dancing together for his amusement. And why wouldn't they want to entertain him? He's been so generous to their kind...

Although he'd never admit it to the insufferable Moldovian, he had indeed amassed a huge quantity of leeches in the attic above his practice. He constructed a towering vat of copper, where his specimens lurk, churning in cloudy freshwater from Algernon Creek. He doesn't waste them on traditional bloodletting because most of his jabbering patients are not worthy of those intimate suckers and the vampirism that follows. Instead, he feeds his parasites the fresh, hot blood of cats and dogs, and has a pack of street children hunting for strays to bring to him night and day. It's surprising what a starving lad might do for a hunk of bread and a bit of salted cod.

No, his leeches are reserved for much greater work than bloodletting. Something born from bloat, but sentient, teachable, and destined to become his magnum opus in the world of medicine. Small, uncultured minds will not be able to understand. But those willing to transcend to a more primeval way of thinking...

They'll marvel, they'll learn, and perhaps in time, his babies will usher in a new religion.

⚜

Carron doesn't think of the room as a morgue, for it is too generous a term. Earthen floors and stone walls drip with algae, a fetid dungeon fit for the Dark Ages, but the best place to stack up bodies like cordwood since the largest cathedral in the city is right above it. It made sense to have the bodies stored on sacred ground, but the odor is so foul that the surgeon is almost dizzy. He was used to dealing with the most suppurating wounds, but the death scent down here is different. It's not fresh, but deeply ingrained, like the rot has crawled up through the stones of the root cellar and tangled itself like vines. He holds a handkerchief smeared in theriac to his nose and mouth as he heads toward it, but even a combination of fifty-five medicinal herbs cannot keep the rancid taste from tickling his throat.

A catacomb hive lurks just beneath the city, and the surgeon travels through it to reach his room. He wouldn't be caught dead trafficking in a charnel house in broad daylight while the church is full of parishioners. He comes only at night when the night work needs doing, and in such cases, the dark can be a concealing friend.

The man who leads him is diminutive, no larger than four feet tall, and Carron thinks he must have some rupture in the brain, for no sane individual would be able to stand it down here for long. A smell like this one eats through sanity, and you'd be prone to lose yourself and end up joining the corpses. When the little man turns and shows the rosebud crater where his nose once was, eaten to the core by unchecked syphilis, the surgeon thinks that it's no great reach to assume that he's taken a few dead lovers in his time.

Carron has seen this ruin of a face many times before, but he's always tempted to press his index finger into that dripping sinus hole to see how deep the putrefaction goes. Call it professional curiosity…

"You is a queer one, Carron. But I ain't never met a sawbones that wasn't queer."

The two men walk together through the dank chamber, bodies piled up on stone shelves with thin sheets covering them, most of the sheets stained in a mixture of red and yellow as the blood seeps out and the fatty tissue breaks down.

"Always shaking fingers at the graverobbers, but here you is with me again, lining me pockets and wanting heads. I done sold you four good heads in the span of just a few months. And none of them bad ones that the fruit flies been hatching in. Good clean heads, them souls not a few hours outta their sickbeds--"

"Do not compare me to the heathens that sneak with their lanterns digging in the mud for jewels and gold teeth," Carron interrupts. "You receive a handsome payment for your discretion. My research is revolutionary, and the details would confound you, Miles. Worry less about my affairs and more about your footing on these mossy stones."

Miles guffaws, the sound echoing through the chamber, and every bat and spider hiding in the vicinity trembles at the disturbance. "These slippery paths is marked on the back of me hand, sawbones! Wot you want them all for? Can you at least say that?"

"The others were not quite right. There is fine tuning to be done. But I'm close, Miles. Closer than I've ever been before."

"Well, I tell you wot, I could sweeten the pot. A bit more coin and

I'll fetch you three arms, two stout legs, and a whole torso that's still warm to the touch. Ain't that a bargain?"

"I've no use for limbs. *Sarx* lacking soul. Flesh bereft of spirit. I need only heads, and I need them intact."

The little man shrugs and continues onward, the guttering torches on the walls painting the cadavers in harsh firelight. They reach a small circular section of the catacombs, and Miles approaches a rectangular indentation in the stone wall. He pulls the sheet back from the body that is at rest within, and Carron finds himself looking down at a young man with curly black hair and skin so pale it is almost translucent. The surgeon fixates on the eyelashes, so lush and long, they are close to feminine.

"Beaut of a boy, wasn't he? Lived in the slums and drank too much piss water from a bad well, from what I was told. Cholera. Nasty way to go, but the head is still as fresh as flowers. Think he'll do?"

Carron takes hold of the boy's gaunt cheeks and moves his head from side to side, looking for any superficial damage or fractures in the skull. There's not a single dent or blemish. If not for the pallidity, the boy could be mistaken for having fallen into a deep slumber.

"More than sufficient. Perhaps the best head you've shown me so far."

The surgeon turns and places a small sack of coins into the caretaker's hand, and Miles beams while scratching at the open wound on his face.

"Listen closely, Miles. When you hack this one off, not a bit of damage from the neck up. I want it to be a precise cut. If you can manage that, I'll double the sum, and you'll receive the other half after delivery."

"That's a square deal, sawbones. I'll have it sent to ya' in a burlap sack, and I'll take her off nice and delicate."

Carron nods and heads off in the direction the two men entered from, and Miles remains there, reaching for the pitted hatchet that's tucked into his belt. He tests the blade with the pad of his thumb, and then he makes her whistle through the air. It's like chopping meat for a pie, and when the decapitation is finished, the stump of neck is so perfectly aligned that you'd think the boy lost his head to a guillotine.

The head sits mounted beneath a coiled pipe referred to as a *worm*, something Carron purchased from a moonshiner in the forested hills far beyond the city limits. The clipped jugular is attached to the worm, and the worm curls off in two directions - one length of pipe jutting down into the vat of agitated leeches and the other into an old porcelain clawfoot tub on the opposite side of the room. The tub is a broiling broth of unstable alchemy, something the surgeon has dabbled in secretively for decades now. It's a lost art, medieval chemistry, and the fumes rising from his stew are so powerful that he must wear multiple rags tied across his mouth and nose, lest he drop to the floor with burnt lungs.

The ingredients are vague and caustic, but the intention is to awaken a different level of cognition in the leeches. The animals have thirty-two brains in each of their segments, and Carron's fumes are meant to open them up wider like faucets, creating something like a superleech, capable of animating the severed head and making it the ultimate willing host.

Carron uses a large wooden ladle to stir the contents of his broth, milk of sulfur, bitumen, gypsum, King's yellow, and other obscure herbs that form a recipe so toxic it makes the daisies in his windowsill wilt and blacken down to the roots.

He approaches the head, that beaut of a boy, and he studies all of the incisions and alterations he made after its arrival. The eyes were removed, and the orbital sockets scooped out, along with the entire lower mandible and both upper and lower sets of teeth. What remains are dark ragged holes, and the skin flaps unencumbered by restrictive bone. He left the skull, but he bored holes into it through the scalp from multiple angles, creating entry points to make the brain accessible. For his work to be a success, the leeches must interface with the brain on a biological level, the perfect marriage of dead flesh and supercharged organisms.

The fumes from the tub have reached the leeches in their towering home, and the effect is immediate. The copper vat starts to churn, and the parasites are driven to the point of near madness, their combined movements causing the enormous vat to shake from side to side. Carron is flitting from instrument to instrument, checking his measurements, making small adjustments, and all the while, his belt of scalpels and knives creates jagged music as he races through his makeshift attic lab.

Leeches begin to shoot up through the coiled pipe, fast as bullets, slithering through the jugular and into the skin of the head, suckling and slurping it from the inside. They flop through the cratered eyeholes and it takes mere seconds for them to discover the drilled skull chasms that lead down to the brain. The leeches burrow enthusiastically, and they attach to the moist gray matter, suckling at it, nibbling with vigor, the fumes of alchemy infused in wiggling black bodies that cannot resist this sole chance to evolve.

An unnatural luminance is born in the infested head, the glowing green of swamp gas, but as the flesh starts to engorge, Carron panics, thinking it'll explode, and the experiment will end as another failure for him. But the head does not explode. The flesh turns malleable, and it continues to pulsate and engorge, but instead of splitting like an overripe gourd, the head grows, enlarging and pumping up from the inside, thousands of leeches working their dark mechanics in the brain, jumpstarting a resurrection into something entirely unheard of in the scientific community.

Carron stumbles back, and he realizes he's weeping in triumph.

119

The head is doubling in size, and now tripling, a gargantuan mass of tissue, the open mouth flapping like a sail, the once empty eyes now holding black pupils of balled up and wiggling leeches. Soon the surgeon is dwarfed, and he realizes the attic cannot contain what he has brought into existence. The head detaches from the coiled pipe, the jugular trailing as a means of propulsion, and it begins to rise and rise, smacking up against the ceiling, crushing the rafters, turning the tin roof above to dust and shrapnel.

It's the size of a hot air balloon now, floating freely and stirring a euphoria in Carron, airborne not with helium, but with some new component the leeches have introduced, a means of flight denied to them in their past lives lurking in river muck and taking what paltry blood meals they could. This is the next phase of leech evolution. This is what Carron always knew the parasites *could* become if given the proper love and care...

He flees down the narrow staircase, abandoning his attic, the lab tumbling in on itself behind him. Chemicals burst in vials and some level of combustion occurs, because as soon as Carron reaches the cobblestones, the entire building is a bright blaze of fire, a halo of noxious swamp green hanging above all.

The surgeon does not care. He is awestruck, because there floating just above the rooftops is his beautiful balloon, his legion of leeches together as one, moving with the delicacy of a hummingbird seeking nectar in the springtime. He can smell it even from his place below, a sweet mixture of sulfur, baked blood, and renewed and repurposed skin.

The pedestrians on the street take notice, and Carron could not be prouder. He listens to the gasps and the shouts. He watches women faint into the arms of their husbands. This is ascension. This is creation.

This is what it means to father a demigod.

꧁꧂

Carron walks the streets like a man doused in morphine, a smile plastered across his face. His big, beautiful balloon unfurls a string down to him, the leeches forming something like a link, and he holds the squishy end of it, making sure not to squeeze too tightly. It warms his heart that they want to be close to their maker. Far above where it floats, the engorged head continues to grow, and it makes a sound too, a persistent groaning of fumes seeking release. Occasionally it belches out a warm torrent of that swamp gas to the streets below. The vegetation yellows where it touches, and the water is brought to a boil.

People gape at him and his balloon. They cross themselves in the thresholds of their rowhouses. Judgmental peasants, but how can such uneducated souls appreciate the divine even when it's presented to them?

The scorn seems to bother his balloon on an instinctual level, for the leeches are self-aware now, and they don't comprehend the fear and disgust being shown them. The floating head begins to cry big fat leeches from its ragged eyeholes, and it is like a midnight rain from the heavens. They fall and explode in the streets, blood globs spraying, but when a leech teardrop hits a human, the parasite is quick to squirm up the body and into their screaming mouth.

What happens next is a medical marvel. The body of the host bloats as the leech affixes to the brain, their eyes pop out and roll down their cheeks, and their teeth tumble free to clatter against the cobblestones. A look of absolute euphoria crosses over the face of the host, and the body begins to float. They rise and circle Carron's wondrous balloon, tiny moons orbiting a gas giant planet, and a level of peace is obtained that the surgeon has never seen before in his adult life. The leeches know nothing of war, murder, and pain. They know only of the warm bloat that comes with blood, and how they've always dreamed of taking to the skies.

The dark rain continues, a torrential downpour of living leeches, and with each new host obtained, the balloon's congregation grows. Carron passes in front of the cathedral, and he recognizes Miles stumbling down the front steps as he stares up at the head hovering beneath the clouds.

"I knew not wot you was doing in that attic, Carron. If I had known this was your goal with that head, I'd have spat in yer eyes! You're a mad hatter drunk on poison tea. Call off yer' sky dog. Call it off before it kills us all!"

Carron favors Miles with a smile so dark and dazed, it makes the little man stagger back a step. It's clear the surgeon has lost his marbles, and the ones that remain are cracked and rolling haphazardly in his head.

"There's no death here, Miles. My balloon is as innocent as a babe fresh from the womb. What you're witnessing up there is transcendence. Leeches learning how to feel. Leeches learning how to love…"

Miles begins to bark like an angry dog, spittle flying out from his lips and phlegm from the hole where his nose should be. "Put an end to it, sawbones! Unmake that forsaken thing…"

Carron pulls a rusted bone saw from his belt and reaches out to grab hold of the back of the little man's head, spinning him around and putting the ragged teeth of the saw close to his Adam's apple. The surgeon gently tilts Miles's head upward, forcing him to look at the balloon. "Shh. Stifle your hysterics. Let me show you how to join them…"

The surgeon whispers up into the sky, and the balloon turns to listen.

"Take him, sweet one. Help him to understand."

The balloon lowers, and Carron studies the facial features with rapture. Eyeholes like squirming black islands, pouting mouth of formless flapping lips that spill over with swampy brine, weeping like Christ on the cross, leeches tumbling down pallid cheeks.

It gets so close that Carron's head swims, and the sound of its internal gurgling drowns out Miles's shrieks. It stretches its mouth wide and vomits a whole waterfall of leeches onto Miles, the parasites entering the man from every orifice he has to offer. It takes mere seconds for him to bloat, for his eyes to pop and his teeth to crumble, and Carron releases him so he can drift skyward. *When you circle the balloon, you don't need to see, and you don't need to eat. You just need to feel...*

"Be free, Miles. Be free."

The balloon ascends again, and it's so humongous now that it blots out the sun. There is no natural light left in the city. It has been eclipsed, and what's left is everlasting dark. Carron finds it peaceful. His balloon is honest, compassionate, and the leeches know a better way.

He allows his hand to slip from the string he's been holding onto. The head pauses in midair, and it turns to look at him. He must look so small to it up there, creation having surpassed its maker. The balloon frowns, a frown that spans the length of multiple cornfields, and Carron can tell it's unsure of itself.

"We are a flawed species, sweet one. I've cut so many of us open, and there's nothing inside but hollow meat and an absence of spirit. We had our turn, and we've botched it. We cannot change unless you show us. Will you be merciful to your dear old dad?"

The surgeon unclasps his belt and lets it drop. The scalpels and knives fall to the dirt, and he's glad to be free of their burden. He drops to his knees, kneeling and smiling up at his big, beautiful balloon. After a time, the balloon learns to smile back.

"I'm ready."

The surgeon closes his eyes and opens his mouth, hoping dearly that the forecast calls for rain. He feels a plump, warm leech land on his tongue, and he eagerly swallows. It's better than opium. It's better than sex.

A sickly-sweet flood of joy engorges his body, and Hubert Carron ascends to join his beloved balloon.

WOMAN OF THE WHITE COTTAGE

Rebecca Jones-Howe

The first time Mary saw the man through her cottage window, he was cutting down a tree with an axe. The tree had already slipped out of the earth during the last storm. For weeks it lay there, growing mushrooms at its base. Leaves twisted off the branches and rustled against her cottage windows like fingers tapping, trying to get her.

The man made good work of the tree. His axe slipped easily into the trunk, severing limbs and revealing the wood's rotted insides. He exerted so much effort, yet made his task seem so easy at the same time.

Mary found herself fixated. She stood at her door, her flesh prickling hot with the rash that kept her isolated in her cottage, often for days on end. Normally the rash affected her hands, but now the burn shifted to her chest, making her heart beat sparks inside of her. With that prickling came a desire. A need.

She made the man a cup of Earl Grey tea and pushed at her screen door. Her hesitant steps sunk into the mud as she crossed her strawberry patch to meet him.

125

"Thank you," he said, lifting the cup to his lips. "You're very kind."

His smile closed the vastness of the sky above her. It made the woods feel a little less expansive. The tea flushed his cheeks and warmed his strong demeanor. Then he handed her back the empty cup, taking notice of the red bumps on her hands.

"It's only a rash," Mary said.

"But what might be the cause?"

Mary took a step back and stumbled, getting dirt on her skirt. "I've always had it," she said. "It comes and goes."

"Can I see?" he asked, reaching out.

Mary hesitated, feeling the prickle in her stomach as she offered herself to him. He ran his fingers over her skin, his grit scratching the itch, if just for a moment.

"It doesn't look very pleasant," he said. "It looks quite aggravating, if I'm honest."

"It drives me mad," she said and withdrew, allowing the man to finish his task. She watched him from the doorstep of her cottage, her grasp clinging to the frame of the door as the man's shoulders stretched the fabric of his linen shirt. He chopped the limbs off the lifeless trunk. He twisted off the shorted branches with bare hands. Then he carried the trunk away, his head heavy, his steps leaden down the long and narrow path that led into town.

Once he was gone, Mary pressed her lips to the mug where the man had drunk. She could taste him in the bergamot.

⚜

Mary didn't go into town often.

She avoided it if she could. She hated the open sky and the voices that echoed around her. The townspeople had made a spectacle of her for being childless and alone. Not to mention the rash, its shameful red always reappearing whenever she found herself under the scrutiny of others.

A part of her wanted to follow the man, but her better instincts told her to remain inside the enclosure of her white cottage, protected for as long as her food and water lasted.

She kept the cottage clean. She always swept, always washed, always brought in cut flowers to dry. She hung them upside down in her windows, their delicate petals further preventing the curious residents in town from looking in.

The second time the man came, Mary knelt in her garden, turning grapefruit rinds over her strawberry patch in order to trap the slugs.

"Do you have any more?" he asked. "I do love a ripe grapefruit."

Mary looked back to her cottage door, her mouth drying. She wound her fists over her sleeves, trying to hide the growing rash from his gaze.

The man reached into his coat pocket. "This might help your hands," he said, holding out a bottle of salve for her to take.

Despite the burn, she allowed the sun's glare to grace her skin.

"Nathaniel Edwards," he said. "I recently moved into town."

"Oh," she said, wondering if this was the reason why he'd taken the log, to build his own cabin. It was a romantic thought, a silly one. Even she knew that. Nobody would build a cabin with an infected log. "My name is Mary," she said.

"Yes," he said, his smile deepening. "The people in town have spoken of you."

"Hopefully not all bad things," she said.

Nathaniel cocked his head and took a step closer, glancing down at the grapefruit rind in her hand. "They joke that you're a witch, but we all know witches are purely fiction. Is that not the truth, Mary?"

His charm pulled the warmth from her hands. The prickle worked up her chest and into her face, her cheeks, her lips. His kindness turned her caution into a smile, which she found herself unable to hide.

⊶⊷

The third time, Nathaniel came to her at night. A rock tapped against the window and Mary climbed out of bed to find him standing before the cottage with a bundle of hand-picked wildflowers. Mary clutched at the curtains.

She was hesitant to tell him that the salve he'd given her had made the rash worse. The red spread across her chest and her belly. It traveled down and festered an itch in her loins.

Nathaniel approached the door, his mud-soaked boots weighing over the doorstep. She liked his throat up close. She liked his swallow.

His Adam's Apple bobbed in the most neglected part of her.

She pulled the door open and let him inside.

⊶⊷

Jezebel.

He left dirt in her bed. Dirt in the sheets, dirt on the floorboards. He left a trail of footprints out the door and down the long narrow path that led into town. Mary watched him leave, the emptiness of the forest creeping closer, reaching into her space to touch her.

She slammed the door shut and locked it. Then she cleaned the dirt off her floor, frantic, her limbs shaking. She scrubbed and polished and rinsed Nathaniel's scent out of her sheets, still hearing his husky whisper calling her *Jezebel* in the peak of lust.

After putting on a clean cotton dress, she found a vase for the flowers he'd picked her. She arranged them nicely on the dining table, blinking at the white blossoms until sleep took her, took the rash away, made everything normal again.

128

Nathaniel didn't show again for a while.

For days.

Mary sat restlessly at the window, craving the comfort of release. She scratched at the rash through her dress, willing herself to step beyond her property and toward the river where she first saw him. The riverbank sucked at the heels of her boots, threatening to pull her into the earth. She dipped her iron kettle into the cool water but slipped and got her white dress dirty, her hands dirty. She wiped at her face and got mud on her cheek.

Somebody coughed behind her.

"There you are, dear Jezebel."

She swooned, her body giving, pleading, screaming until the grit of his hands scratched all of her itch away. She cried tears of relief, but Nathaniel only left more dirt behind.

After he left, the rash returned.

Mary scrubbed and swept until her chest tightened. She shook the sand out of her sheets and climbed back into bed, still feeling the grains of earth between her toes. She fell asleep staring at the severed flowers on the kitchen table, their petals still lively and reaching for the light.

Mary went into town on Saturday.

The people were in the streets, moving from shop to shop, passing glances. Mary kept her chin down but her will strong. In the general store, she bought ingredients to make a lemon cake: flour and sugar and baking soda, a little bottle of vanilla extract. She pulled the cork off and savored its strength. She licked the top of the bottle, tasting him.

Lost in the moment, she tilted the bottle and took a drink.

The shopkeeper gasped.

"I-I'm sorry," Mary said. "I was lost in thought."

The bell above the shop door rang and she turned to see Nathaniel. Her heart fluttered and she smiled, her teeth showing. Too blunt, too eager.

He didn't mirror her delight. His lips parted, but he averted his gaze, turning instead for the canned goods.

Mary swallowed. She tried to breathe but her lungs ached.

The shopkeeper then cleared his throat, earning Nathaniel's attention. "A quick word, Doctor?"

The other patrons shuffled as Nathaniel's footsteps worked across the wooden floorboards. Their sneering whispers all spoke her name.

Mary. Oh, Mary.

Mary stumbled, unable to pull her sleeves over the growing rash. Her fingers slipped from the bottle of vanilla, which rattled over the wood floor, its dark liquid sputtering from the mouth like an open wound.

Whispers built into a storm. They sounded like rain against the windows. Mary turned for the shop door, her limbs stiffening when one of the female patrons blocked her path.

"You see, Doctor!" the woman said, pointing. "The red is on her neck now!"

Nathaniel. His name.

Doctor. His title.

"H-he, he cleared a tree by the river," Mary stuttered. "He brought me medicine, though it only seemed to make things worse—"

Nathaniel shook his head. "I am afraid you have me confused with someone else, miss." He forced a wide smile and extended his hand. "Mary, was it?"

Mary's chest flushed and she pulled at the collar of her dress, trying to scratch at the itch. She dropped the flour, the salt, the baking soda. A mountain of white piled at her feet. "I-I thought y-you wanted to help me."

Nathaniel's gaze darkened, focusing in on Mary and the spectacle she now was. Whispered fluttered. Laughter sounded. She felt the voices crawling beneath her skin.

"Mary, the townspeople are very concerned—"

"He-he is lying!" Mary insisted. "He knocked on my door and he came inside."

Jezebel.

Nathaniel shook his head, stepping closer. "Please, Mary, there's no need embarrass me with your wild fantasies."

"He fancied me!" Mary shrieked. "I was sure of it!"

Behind him, mouths opened into blackness. Gasps vibrated against her eardrums like gusts of wind.

Strumpet. Harlot. Hysterical.

Mary stepped back, the heel of her shoe slipping in the spilt flour. She left footprints behind her, a white spiral that wound through the shop as Nathaniel tried to reach her before she fainted.

She gasped, her breaths involuntary. Her skin prickled. Her heart paced.

White walls.

A white ceiling.

Sunlight beamed through the window, but the window wasn't hers.

The wires of the bed poked against her back. She rolled her head away from the glare to the shadow of a man. This time, he was the one in white.

A white shirt. A white coat. A bottle of white smelling salt, which he pulled away from her face.

"Hello, Mary," Nathaniel said.

Mary adjusted to the room, glancing from white wall to white wall, bordered with white moulding, clinical, unlike her cottage, which she'd accented with lace and dried flora. In this room, there was a dresser. There was a chair and a light.

A nurse stood in the open doorway, carrying a metal tray with a syringe.

"Where am I?" Mary tried to sit up but a set of leather restraints caught her wrists and ankles. She twisted against the bindings, but they were tethered to the edges of the bed. "You did this? You brought me here?"

"I work here, Mary," he said. "I'm the new doctor, Dr. Edwards, and it would benefit you greatly if you referred to me as such."

She shook her head, tried to find the truth in his eyes but his gaze only hardened over her shaking figure, buried in the starched fabric of the hospital gown.

"You lied to me," she said.

"I didn't lie to you."

"Let me go!" She turned to the nurse, her throat tightening as she struggled. "I don't belong here! He tricked me! He came to me! He laid with me!"

Dr. Edwards leaned in closer and touched his hand to the burning rash on her bound wrist. "I promise you are safe, Jezebel. I am going to make you better."

Mary opened her mouth. Her cries echoed in the empty room until the nurse came forward with the needle.

Dr. Edwards picked it off the tray.

"No, please!"

"You need rest, Mary." He grabbed her arm and the pierce felt like nothing, like calm.

The drugs slipped into the resistance inside of her.

It was so easy to fall asleep.

The nurse roused her in the morning.

"Dr. Edwards insisted that you have a private room," she said, undoing the bindings from Mary's limbs. "He has high hopes for your treatment here, and so do I."

The nurse smiled too hard, as though trying to make a friend. "We all hope to learn a lot about treating women such as you."

Jezebel.

"I'm not a bad person," Mary insisted.

The nurse sighed and glanced at the rashes working up her arm. "You have been a subject of gossip for quite some time, Mary. I think it is about time to make a change."

Mary shook her head, not wanting to imagine a life beyond her cottage and its familiarity. Yet she was here now, in an asylum, in a different white room that felt too clean and too sanitized. It smelled of bleach and ammonia. The sheets scratched when she rolled out of bed. Her gown burned at her skin.

"Let us get you some breakfast, Mary."

The nurse led Mary though the maze of corridors to the cafeteria. She pulled out a chair among the other women who were supposed to be hysterical like her. None of them looked like Mary or acted like Mary. One of the women cradled a doll that she referred to as Mary. The woman pretended to nurse the doll, but then turned and smashed the doll's face on the table.

Another woman laughed.

Another woman cried.

"You are quite alright, Mary," the nurse said. "Just listen and obey, and soon you'll be home again."

Mary took her spoon and tried to eat her porridge without shaking, but she couldn't keep her hand calm, couldn't breathe when her chest was pocked so red with shame.

She wanted to tell the nurse that she wasn't like these women. She was just lonely. Desperate. Scared.

She thought Nathaniel was trying to help her.

She thought he meant well.

Her gaze wandered, but ultimately settled upon the tiled floor, which was marked with glistening trails that wove between the tables and through the doorways.

The nurse walked away but didn't leave a trail, and Mary dropped her spoon in her bowl, suddenly sick, suddenly feeling the need to scratch at her skin. She rose from the table and found the clearest line of slime to follow.

It led her out of the cafeteria and down a long corridor, down a set of stairs, down another hallway full of windows. The heat beamed in. She squinted and shielded her eyes before opening a door that led into the auditorium.

Her breath reverberated in the vast open space.

Paranoid. Afraid.

The beams of the ceiling rose over her like the open sky, but she kept her head low, her bare feet flat over the floorboards. She hurried across the empty span of the floor and found another door, which led to another hallway full of open offices that glared like eyes.

Then she heard *his* voice, speaking to another. "I firmly believe that I have found a most suitable candidate for my studies. She exhibits hysterical symptoms, both mental and physical. I'll surely make publication writing of her treatment."

Mary scratched at the heat, her moan echoing.

Then, a shadow.

Nathaniel startled when he spotted her.

"Jezebel. What are you doing here?"

Her heart raced. She turned, only to hear his footsteps hammering the tiled floor behind her, a white coat in pursuit.

She ventured back the way she thought she'd come, pushing through the door and into a different hallway. Behind the next door waited another office wing. Behind the next door, a patient wing.

"Mary!" he called.

She hurried, her chest burning at the sound of her name. She twisted another knob and found a stairwell.

Mary stood at the top, her fists gripping the wrought iron railing as the sunlight burned at her back. She leaned over the railing and stared at the floors below, imagining herself getting to the bottom faster than anyone could chase her. She imagined her body at the bottom, broken and torn, weathering into dirt atop the marble tiles.

Such an unnatural place for one to die.

The door opened behind her. It wasn't Dr. Edwards, but the nurse. "Mary, dear, you have to return to your room. You cannot be running about the facility like this. You'll get yourself lost."

"I'm not lost," Mary said.

The nurse took her elbow, but Mary wrestled herself away and went down the stairwell herself, the friction of the iron railing burning beneath her palm. She glanced upward at the nurse who followed, only to crash into another body.

She smelled bergamot.

"You sure look lost to me, Mary," Nathaniel said. His gaze overwhelmed her, just like the trees in the forest. She stumbled back to see the nurse, whose smile had faded and given way to judgement.

"I am *not* lost," she said again. "There is *nothing* wrong with me!"

"Oh, Mary," the nurse said, her gaze lingering upon her ripe red flesh.

Nathaniel's grasp tightened over her shoulder. "Get her a jacket," he said.

"You're a fallen woman," he said.

The orderlies snickered as they twisted the white sleeves around her frame.

"You hurt yourself. You've shamed yourself with your hysterics."

Mary shook her head, struggling to breathe. "I did nothing!" she gasped. Behind her, the orderlies tied up the back like corset knots, yanking her breath from her lungs.

The doctor leaned in closer. "But you let me in, Jezebel. You *did* do something to bring yourself shame."

Another bout of laughter.

Jezebel.

"Do not call me that."

Nathaniel leaned in closer and smiled. Behind him, the nurse entered and placed a new stainless-steel tray on the table. On it was a new needle, drawn full of relief. Mary twisted in her binds.

"Beg for it," Nathaniel said.

The sight of it flushed her, made her itchy, made her writhe.

Everyone could see it, even through the white of the straight-jacket.

Jezebel. Jezebel. Jezebel.

"I want to go home," she cried.

"You cannot control yourself at home," Dr. Edwards said.

The nurse observed Mary's tear-stained face and swallowed.

"You knocked," Mary said. "You knocked on my door and you made it worse."

"Would you like a *different* door, Mary? A padded cell, perhaps?"

"You brought me flowers! You left your dirt in my bed!"

The orderlies whispered just like the people in town.

"Stop—"

"Beg!" he screamed, reaching for the needle. "Beg for sleep! Beg for relief!"

Mary screamed, watching as the nurse left the room. The orderlies forced her back onto the bed, wrestling her ankles into the bindings, ratcheting a strap over the itchiest part of her chest. Sand scraped into her flesh, grains embedding, settling, making it hard to breathe.

"Please!"

The needle slipped into her skin, and the drug filled her veins, feeling like earth burying her.

⁂

Porridge. Its blandness tasted like dirt on Mary's tongue.

Beside her, the woman with the doll lifted spoonfuls against its stitched smile.

"Take it, Mary," she said.

Mary traced the glistening lines on the cafeteria floor. They were fresh morning trails of slime, which her eye followed toward the group of orderlies snickering in the corner.

Slugs, she thought.

Whenever she ran out of grapefruit rinds, she had to resort to using salt to keep the slugs from her strawberries. She hated killing, but a part of her couldn't help but watch as their bodies twisted and contorted against the grains.

The nurse approached and touched her shoulder.

"It is time for your examination, Mary," she said, taking her by the arm. She led her down the maze of hallways and doors and stairways and into a room containing a wall of cabinets and a metal table with stirrups.

From one of the cabinets, the nurse pulled out a tray full of sanitized metal instruments.

Mary swallowed. "There is nothing wrong with me."

But the nurse frowned this time. "Your rash has gotten worse since you were admitted," she said. "Dr. Edwards needs to figure out what is causing it and he cannot do that without examining you." She set the tray down on the cart and motioned for Mary to climb on the examination table. The cold metal creaked beneath her weight.

Then the door opened, and Nathaniel entered, again in his white coat, with a pen in his shirt pocket and a stethoscope around his neck.

"Mary," he said with a smile, glancing at the table before dismissing the nurse.

Mary wanted to shake her head but thought of the straight-jacket, of the restraints and the orderlies. The nurse left, her lips pursed. Dr. Edwards approached with no words. He slipped his hand beneath the neckline of her gown, exposing her chest to the clinic's cold air.

"My, how flushed you are," he said, pressing the end of the stethoscope to her chest.

She gripped over the edge of the table as her paranoia beat into his ears.

She moaned a little.

He smiled a little.

"Take a deep breath," he said, gripping her shoulder, ruining what careful intimacy she could remember with his cold commands. The rash burned up her neck and onto her cheeks. She shut her eyes, allowing the tears to break through.

Nathaniel turned to the tray of instruments.

"Easy, Mary," he said, easing a tongue depressor past her lips, forcing her to open her mouth for him.

He forced new intimacy, shining a light into her eyes, a scope in her ears. He pressed his fingers against her neck and her stomach, her wrists and her groin, leaning in so close, so tense, his attention solely focused on how her body betrayed her.

He pushed on her chest to ease her backward, but she resisted.

"Lay down, Mary," he ordered, reaching for the speculum.

She shook her head and met his gaze, the one that once made her feel like a different woman, a relieved woman. In the sterile room, his hardened stare proved he would never be the same man who entered her cottage again.

"I want to go home," she pleaded.

"You cannot, Mary. Not until I say so." He gripped at her thigh and yanked her leg into the stirrup.

The metal shook, rattling in the empty space of the room. Mary braced herself on the table's edge.

"You know what will happen if you refuse to comply," he said. "The orderlies already know how to tame you. Do I need their help, Mary, or can we keep this matter between us?"

Jezebel.

She stared at the ceiling, drawing a shaky breath as she lifted her other leg out of limbo and into the second stirrup. For him, she parted her knees. For herself, she allowed him back inside of her body, this time with the sterile steel that widened and revealed. He probed and shone a light and wrote his impressions down on her chart, all while she held her breath and tried not to cry as the burn worked inside of her.

When he was done, he sighed and pulled the speculum out, placing it back onto the tray of sullied metal, the blades glistening in the light.

⚜

It was the nurses now, who stared and grimaced when they saw her.

Jezebel.

Mary ate her porridge and tried to think back to her white cottage, the isolation of it, the notoriety of it. Did she really have other men there, like the nurses said? Did she lure them there with tea and fruit and freshly baked cakes?

Have other hands mauled her, ruined her?

Was she nothing but dirt?

The nurses' laughter drove her from her seat and out of the cafeteria. All she wanted was a place away from the sunlight, which was all the asylum provided. Its myriad of uncovered windows exposed her flesh to the shame of the sun.

None of the other patients paid her any mind. They all twisted themselves through the corridors, all of them lost women in their own spirals. Mary wondered if this truly was madness: isolation and fear left to fester for too long.

Mary followed a trail of slime down a new stairwell and through a heavy metal door. It led beneath the earth to a dark brick tunnel. Long pipes stretched like sinew down the hall and into the unknown. The pipes whispered, full of hot steam that misted the narrow space. Mary thought she would choke in it, but the only other option was to return to the sun and the glare, so she shut the door behind her and continued.

She ventured deep, thinking of the shame of her examination, the feeling of Dr. Edwards' observation, the scratch of his pen when he wrote on her chart. She scraped her nails at the brick walls, lit by single bulbs that appeared sporadically down the corridor. Her bare feet slipped into the puddles, into the mud.

Down a fork in the tunnel, she heard humming. A song.

Mary, Mary, quite contrary…

She willed herself to go on, clawing her way further, turning corners, turning her head to make sure she wasn't followed.

"Mary! Oh, Mary! How *does* your garden grow?"

She'd found the woman with the doll, crouched beside a locked gate. The woman looked up at her, flashing a smile of missing teeth. She held up the doll to Mary, made the doll wave at Mary.

"Would you like to see Mary's garden?"

The woman pointed at a box full of soil on the ground. Mary had to squint to see through the steam, but what lingered in the dirt was a cluster of red mushrooms. The woman plucked one from the soil and brought it to her lips. Then she picked up another and held it out as an offering.

"If they knew about Mary's garden, they would take it away."

Mary shook her head.

"They call you Mary," the woman continued, "but you can't be Mary. *She* is called Mary." The woman rocked the doll and hummed.

Mary twisted her fingers into her gown, prying at the neckline, trying not to scratch.

"He calls me Jezebel," she said, her voice low.

The woman smiled. "Jezebel is a pretty name. A poisonous name." She offered the mushroom again.

This time, Mary took it, keeping the spore cradled in the warmth of her palm as she carried it back upstairs and into the light.

She found herself in the recreation hall, where the nurses and the orderlies grabbed at her limbs and brought her back to where she was supposed to be.

In her bed. In her room.

Her sterilized home.

She clutched the mushroom in her palm, protecting it from the light as the orderlies wound her limbs back into the tethers. Her body told her to struggle, but she remembered the woman in the tunnel, who had already informed her that *Mary* no longer existed.

Mary was already dead.

She stared at the window, at the glare of the sun outside, which shone over the asylum and the trees and the single road that led back into the village, and eventually, back to her cottage, where she had hidden herself for too long.

Further down the horizon, she could see clouds of grey.

"Please," she begged. "Please help me."

⚜

At night, the door opened and a white figure entered. Rain pattered against the window and Mary drew in a breath of the saturated air. Nathaniel's shoes squeaked over the tiles. In his fist, he held a batch of gathered flowers. He tossed them on her figure, as though her bed were a grave.

"Do you know why you belong here?" he asked.

Jezebel.

He knelt over the bed and released her from her tethers. He leaned in close and pressed his lips against her ear.

"You were isolated, Mary. Hysterical. Childless and alone and without purpose." His words hardened, raining spittle on her cheek. "I took pity on you, and you mistook that pity for lust."

"I mistook it for kindness," she cried, pushing him back.

"Only a whore would mistake the kindness of a well-established doctor, Mary."

She shook her head. "I had no idea you were a doctor."

"You are telling me that you *willingly* laid with a stranger?" he said, lips curving into a smirk. "So there must be some truth then, in what the nurses say? Have you bedded one of the orderlies yet?"

All of her wanted to shrink beneath his accusation, but instead she lifted a palm to his chest, wanting to see if he had a beating heart at all.

"You see?" he said, finally standing, stepping away from her reach. He staggered over the floor, slipping in his own trail. "There *is* quite the whore in this house!"

A bead of water dripped down the ceiling and touched her forehead. She shifted on the bed, then forced herself to stand. The floor

142

was slick with rain now. She lifted her gaze to the leak of black on the ceiling, but then the doctor's stare replaced the void.

"You need to rest, Mary."

He approached again and wrestled her back into the bed. He took her face in his hands, pressed his fingers to her skull, trying to reach inside.

"I *had* to fix you, Mary," he seethed. "I am *going* to fix you."

Her chest burned and she imagined his strong hands carrying the dead tree away. He dragged her back to the bed and threw her body atop the mattress, her limbs tired, her will dead, a place where mushrooms could fester.

He watched her chest rise and fall and he ground his jaw in frustration, in disgust.

He turned and left her untethered.

Rain poured in through the leak in the ceiling. It bled into the dirt he left behind, forming a puddle that grew through the night.

In the morning, Mary crawled out of bed, moving on hands and knees over the muddy floor. She opened the bottom drawer of the dresser, gathered handfuls of fresh dirt, and piled it over the crushed mushroom she'd been given. Footsteps sounded in the hall and she pushed the drawer closed just in time.

The nurse stared at moisture on the floor, then glanced up at the ceiling and the black hole that had spread over night.

"My God, Mary. What have you done?"

Mary kept her lips tight.

"Answer me, Mary."

It didn't matter how she answered. She'd never be able to turn the nurse's glare. It only hardened over her, and the nurse grabbed her elbow, dragging her from her room and into the narrow shower hall.

She pried off Mary's gown and forced her beneath the spray of tepid water with a rough-bristled brush and a bar of soap.

"Clean yourself, Mary."

Goosebumps flocked Mary's skin like spores. She shrunk beneath the water and stammered a plea of remorse.

"Clean yourself or I will have to do it for you."

So, Mary took the brush and ran the thick bristles down her arm.

"Not good enough," the nurse said, and she walked into the shower and yanked the brush from Mary's hand, forcing her onto the tiled floor so she could drag the brush down her back. The soap stung against her flesh, made it boil and froth.

"Please! Please!"

But the nurse didn't stop until the burn spread all over, until the rash had spread from her chest to her back. Once dry, Mary was given a new crisp gown, the starched fabric irritating her fresh wounds.

"Let me get the doctor," the nurse said, taking Mary back to her room.

"No, please!" Mary pleaded, but the nurse returned with Nathaniel.

"My goodness, Mary!" he said, gawking at the room. "Look what has become of you." He withdrew another bottle of salve from his pocket, just like the bottle he'd given her before.

This time Mary wasn't given the chance to protest. The nurse held her down while Nathaniel applied the salve to her raw flesh, the chemicals stinging, drawing cries of sorrow that sounded like the shaking leaves in the trees.

He kept her confined to her bed so her skin could heal.

Hours passed with nothing to do but stare out the open door. Orderlies passed and leered, leaving their glistening trails behind. Some even tried to enter her room with a smile and a laugh and the muttering of her new name, but not before one of the nurses shooed them away.

"She is poisonous," they whispered. "Look at how red her skin is."

Day slipped into night, and with the darkness came more clouds and rain.

The black filled the ceiling again, dripping down and forming new puddles on the marble floor.

Dr. Edwards came again. "You are not improving in the least," he said, pressing a thick layer of salve to her skin. "The nurses tell me things, Mary. They tell me what you do, that you leer at the men who pass, just as you did to me."

Mary shook her head.

"I know it resides inside of you," he said. "I saw it inside of you. Surely you must feel it in there, corrupting you."

He scratched at her stomach, his fingers curling, drawing blood.

She twisted against her binds. "Please!" she cried. "Please!"

"This is how you writhed beneath me," he said, pinching her, pulling at her skin like tree bark. "That is just how you begged."

Jezebel!

The rain pummeled the window, a rush of cold that she forced herself to focus on until his hands released her, and he left the room, locking the door behind him, leaving footprints in the dirt.

By morning, the moisture had seeped into her sheets and her pillow. It swelled the joints of the dresser, which allowed the mushroom spores to fester in the warmth of the morning dew. Little red and white blotches peeked out through the dirt and grew.

The nurse turned her nose at the state of Mary's room.

She stepped carefully over the earth and set a tray of food over her lap.

No porridge this time, but a fresh half of a grapefruit, a boiled egg, and a slice of toast. A square of butter slid across the bread, but then the orderlies came and took her by the arms, lifted her out of bed and onto a gurney.

They wheeled her into a pastel yellow room filled with cabinets and machines and a bright light that glared in her face.

Dr. Edwards was already there, his face brimming with determination as he lifted a new needle full of fluid.

"Please," Mary begged.

But he slid the needle into her arm, drawing his lips near and his breath to a whisper. "Jezebel, Jezebel, here on my pedestal, how does your perversion grow?"

The light glared and Mary closed her eyes as she slipped, imagining a strike of lighting burning her isolated white cottage to ash.

⚜

A yellow room.

A glaring light.

Rain pattered against the skylight and Mary turned her foggy head toward the medical table full of bloodied instruments. Among the clamps and tweezers and knives was a tray that held the piece of her that Dr. Edwards had removed.

Her heart thudded, but the red organ glistened on the tray like a full grapefruit scraped clean from its rind.

Mary struggled but her arms were still strapped and splayed. She turned her head. She tried to sit up, though she was only able to lift her chin, peeking at the stitches that held her midsection from splitting. Her skin swelled. Pinched. Burned.

Dr. Edwards walked to the table with a smile, placing his gloved hand to her face, forcing her to look again at the organ again. She squeezed her eyes shut as his voice vibrated against her ear.

"It was just as I thought, Mary. An infected demon with wings."

She tried to shake her head, but he pressed her cheek to the table.

"What do you say, Mary?"

Her vision blurred with tears. She struggled against her bindings but the drugs made her spin, made her sick and dizzy. Her sobs echoed in the hollow room.

"Say it, Mary."

From the depths of her aching lungs, she found the words.

"Thank you, Doctor."

≈

A slug crawled along her window, leaving behind a glistening trail of slime.

The rain leaked through the growing hole in the roof. No one had cleaned her room and it made Mary shiver in its soaked, desolate state. The base of the wooden dresser had started to rot and now the mushrooms chewed at the wood, growing fat and red and bulbous.

The nurse helped Mary sit up in bed, her lip turned in disgust.

"He wants me to die," Mary said.

"Of course not," the nurse said, bringing Mary a tray of breakfast. Another slice of toast. Another boiled egg with a saucer of salt. Another fresh half of grapefruit. "Dr. Edwards has high hopes for your recovery. Now eat before your food spoils."

Mary ate, slipping her hand to the wound that the stitches tried to contain. She imagined the emptiness inside as she slipped each segment of grapefruit past her tongue. The sinews burst and filled her mouth, but she tasted nothing. She applied the salt to her egg and bit into its overcooked flesh. The food piled inside of her belly, agitating her body, and she twisted in the bed and regurgitated compost onto the tiled floor.

Beside her, the nurse recoiled in disgust.

≈

Another storm fueled the night. She got up and wandered the isolated space of her room, pressing her hands to the walls, spreading the dirt across the sanitized surfaces.

Mary, Mary, quite contrary.

She blinked and hobbled, one hand to her tender abdomen as the sound of footsteps started behind her.

She needed to leave.

She was not thriving.

She was not getting better, as Dr. Edwards had hoped for. The footsteps came closer, and she found herself slipping through doors, the asylum a maze of dead-ends and tormenting spirals. She entered the staircase that she'd tried to descend the first day she'd arrived. Rain clawed at the glass windows, glistening under the low light that leaked in from the hall.

"Jezebel!"

His voice.

He yelled in the night, an accusation now, his growl like thunder in the hallway, his heavy steps beating in her chest. She got to the bottom and crept outside the nearest door and into the courtyard.

The rain touched her skin. It chilled the heat inside of her as she darted out into the night, heading for the trees and the narrow gate that led away.

She stared at the road that led back into town. She could run, could escape. She hurried her pace but felt the stitches pulling, thin threads tugging at her stressed skin. Blood seeped down the front of her gown. Her legs wobbled. She doubled over, her bare feet numb in the mud. The rain turned her hair to tendrils, dragging them down her shoulders. The leaves screamed in her ears, but she could still hear her name.

"Jezebel!"

Everyone knew where her cottage was. They would all come, would all call. They all knew who she was. What she was.

She turned to see his coat of white waiting.

She walked toward his voice, her body just as foul as the woods that surrounded her.

⚜

They both made footprints, walking back into the marbled halls of the asylum.

Lights flickered. Doors opened. People stared.

Mary, Mary, quite contrary. How does your garden grow?

Dr. Edwards left her in the care of the nurse, who ducked her beneath the shower again.

"You filthy whore," she said, scrubbing the brush over her skin, making it burn and boil to a poison shade of red.

The storm continued, even after she was led back to her room. Mary buried herself beneath the covers, curled her feet into the dirt in the sheets and sprouted roots.

⚜

The nurse brought a breakfast tray in the morning. On it was another boiled egg and a saucer of salt. No grapefruit, as she had nothing ripe within.

Mary didn't eat the egg, but she kept the salt clutched in her fist. The crystals melted into the heat of her palms. She licked at her fingers, which left her tongue raw and numb and craving sustenance.

She waited, hungry for Dr. Edwards to visit.

His coat was crisp, freshly bleached and starched with the appearance of cleanliness, yet his shoes sank deep into the mud of her room.

"You are truly beyond help, dear Mary." He left behind a glistening trail just like the slugs in her garden, coming for her overturned

149

rind. He wrestled the chair from the vines in the corner and brought it before her bed. "Are you there, Mary?"

Sunlight cut through the window, warming the earth.

It was still her instinct to clean, but she grinned beneath his attention, slipping her bare foot into the mud as she crept toward him. She curled her toes over the black leather of his shoe.

Nathaniel sat up straight in his chair. "Control yourself, Mary."

She leaned down and gathered a handful of earth. She pressed it between her fingers, ground the soil beneath her nails. She flattened her palm over his white coat, smearing grime over his heart. She pressed hard, gripped at his lapels, climbed over his lap.

His Adam's Apple bobbed in the angriest part of her.

"Mary," he tried.

"Jezebel," she said, slipping her poison fingers past his lips. She pried his mouth open and curled her reach inward, his screams shriveling as the salt burned him inside. "My name is Jezebel."

The Unveiling

Brad Acevedo

The day that Delphine received the letter from the postman should have been a happy occasion. She squealed with delight upon breaking the red wax seal and inspecting the invitation contained within. Silas knew exactly what the correspondence said without reading it. It was a letter that every citizen of Ashfall Hollow hoped to obtain at one point or another. She called him over to share the good news and, as a good and supportive companion, he was obliged to acquiesce.

Silas replaced the *Graverot* specimen he had been studying into a bell jar and set it back into a cabinet. The latest addition to his ever-growing botany collection had started to sprout earlier than intended, and he had been taking careful notes. Silas didn't like to be disturbed in the thick of his studies. If he were to become the foremost expert on Ashfall flora, he needed to to focus. But a special occasion loomed, and he approached the dark-haired woman with a light grin.

"Now, be careful, Silas, don't rip it. I shall have to have it framed and mounted." She grinned proudly.

Silas smirked, ran a prematurely wrinkled hand through graying hair, and studied the letter.

Dear Beloved Citizen,

Please be informed that the recipient of this correspondence is officially invited to attend the Annual Unveiling Ceremony. I respectfully request your presence at my estate to partake in drink, merriment, and the time-honored tradition of presenting one's true self to your fellow citizens. The named individual within this letter is hereby allowed to bring one fellow citizen with them to bear witness to this most momentous occasion.

May the Ash bathe you in blessings,

High Lord Harold DeCinis, Son of Ocul DeCinis

To be Unveiled: Ms. Delphine Anguis

"I- I knew I was ready," Delphine stammered excitedly. "I really did. I could feel it this past year, ready to be removed. Isn't this exciting, Silas?"

He pulled her in and placed a small, whiskery kiss upon her forehead. "It certainly is, dear," he sighed. "But I can't help but notice...an omission."

"An-?" She took the letter back and re-read it carefully. Delphine had been stricken blind by pride and excitement, but with more careful consideration, she noticed what her companion had referred to, or rather the lack thereof. "Oh dear, I'm so sorry. Perhaps next year? But you can still come with me! You'll be my witness and next year, I'll be yours!"

She grinned and he mustered a weak smile in reciprocation. It was an expected blow, but still a damaging one. To not be directly invited to an Unveiling meant that one wasn't prepared to be welcomed into the grand society. Silas's years were advancing, and he didn't know how much longer he could hold out. He was ready, wasn't he? Hadn't he performed a great service for the city, mending and tending to the duel wounds of the High Lords and scraped knees of children alike? No, it had to be some sort of mistake, a rare oversight by the Highest of the High himself.

"Now, don't you fret anymore about this. It is something to celebrate, not to mourn. I'll let you get back to your studies. I have to tell the twins. Maybe they'll be invited themselves! That would be – oh that would -" Delphine continued to stutter, awash in excitement. She blew Silas a kiss and let herself out of his workshop.

He watched her through the opulent front window and observed the swirling hem of her black dress as she strode down the cobblestone streets. She was quite lovely, and he was proud of her. But Delphine deserved a man of honor. Silas picked up the jar of *Graverot* and quickly set it back down. He pulled on his overcoat, picked up his umbrella, and made his way outside. His mind was made up. There were questions to be asked and visits to be made. He would call upon the one who dwelled outside the cusp of common society on the highest dregs of an empire built on ash.

Silas frowned at the ever-falling ash as he made his way outside. He had heard tales of days past when the ash began and blotted out the great shining star above. He'd like to see that star someday, the golden light. But the ash was everywhere. Some even worshipped the ash, but to him it was more of a nuisance.

As Silas hailed a carriage, he shook the gray fall off of his umbrella and sighed as it stained his coat. He climbed aboard and instructed the coachman who responded with a startled look for a brief moment. Silas had expected the reaction. Most townsfolk wouldn't dare approach the DeCinis Manor, but Silas had an advantage, having reattached the foot of the High Lord himself after a particularly eventful hunting trip in his youth. He felt confident, an emotion he had not experienced in some time. Doubt frequently poured into his life, a sullen storm of a gray and forlorn mentality from which no starlight of optimism dare pierce through, not too far removed from the ever-present gray that coated the cobblestone streets and lantern-flame licked twilight haze. At least there was some small light in the dark. It beamed and beckoned with that ever-elusive spark of optimism, emitted from the front gate of the stately manor up ahead. Silas just wanted to be seen, to be known. He placed a coin in the aged hand of the Withered coachman and took the first step towards a future bathed in red and gray.

⚜

Blair answered the massive, black wooden door and Silas cursed silently. He was not fond of Sir DeCinis's butler, a right-hand man of staunch traditionalism who looked down his peaked nose at anyone not born of High Lord blood. "I'm here to see Sir DeCinis," Silas spoke, a bit more meekly than he had intended. "Tell him Dr. Sanguire has come to call."

"I doubt that will be of importance," Blair said stiffly. He tightened the sleeve on the red velvet overcoat he wore for added effect and made to close the door.

"I know that voice. Truly I do!" came a voice from within the manor. It was a masculine and rich voice that echoed of regality and refinement. The Lord of the Manor appeared at the doorway and gently ushered his butler to the side. "Come now, Blair, were it not for this good man, you would have to carry me around on your back all day. I know you would enjoy that!"

"You have no idea, sir," Blair smirked and stepped aside, letting Silas step into the entry hall. It was as opulent as he remembered, all high vaulted brass ceilings, plush purple draperies, and white marble flooring lit by flickering wall-mounted braziers.

Harold DeCinis stepped forward, smelling of cedar, leather, and blood. He reached out with a black gloved hand and clasped Silas's, shaking it with gusto as his gold-laced eyes sparkled. "Dear Doctor, it has been some time. Please step in. May I offer you a drink? I just acquired a splendid vintage from the Maldaken prey-beast fields up north. I hear it's quite bracing." He sucked in a quick breath as if to demonstrate the effect of the drink.

"No, no thank you, my Lord," Silas said respectfully. "I won't be long."

"Well at any rate, pardon the commotion please. We're preparing for the Unveiling Ceremony."

The High Lord gestured inward to the main parlor just beyond the entry hall. Withered servants darted here and there (as swiftly as a Withered one could move, which was not a particularly rapid pace) setting places at gilded tables and dusting various nooks and crannies. Silas took in a sharp breath at the sight. He was always nervous around the Withered. There was something about their gray, gaunt and sunken faces, and the look in their black eyes. No, it was more of the lack of any emotion whatsoever. The poor damned souls (if they had any) were doomed to eons of servitude. They were the remnants of the wild prey-beasts that dwelled in the woods to the north of the city. These were those that the hunters had captured and drained of their very essence, left to waste and not truly live. These were the unfortunates who crossed the wrong side of the High Lords and the Ashen altogether, for death is the end, but to be Withered meant to be eternal. But who would want to live forever only to dwell in supplication and the void of nothingness?

He gathered his thoughts. "My Lord, that is precisely why I am here. As you know, I have been a loyal servant of the city for some time, having helped those who were injured and sick."

"Yes, of course, and we're all grateful," DeCinis said. He paused and scratched at his pale pallor with a sharp black nail.

"My Lord, I have been made aware that the invitations for the Unveiling were recently distributed and, with the utmost respect, I believe I was mistakenly overlooked."

Blair bristled visibly and DeCinis cocked his head to the side. His shoulder length black hair tilted down, a black cascade around slender regal shoulders.

"My dear doctor, to come into my home and insinuate such a thing," DeCinis said, taking in a deep breath. His gold flecked eyes flashed with irritation. "I can assure you there was no mistake. But now... you are of the... Sanguire line, is that correct?"

Silas licked his dry lips and felt a bead of sweat well upon his forehead. He had made a mistake; he shouldn't be here. But he wanted to be seen, to be heard, and so he pressed on. "Yes, sir. That is correct."

"Ah," DeCinis said simply. He gestured to the doctor and walked over to a large oak door off to the left. "Forgive me for one moment?"

He disappeared behind it, leaving a most uncomfortable moment between the doctor, the butler, and the Withered servants. The gray husks paced about silently completing their tasks as Blair gazed back at Silas with silent but thinly veiled contempt. Silas realized he was holding his breath and released it noisily in relief as the High Lord returned. He was carrying a thick, leather bound book and was studying a specific passage. He beckoned Silas closer.

"You see here," DeCinis pointed at the book. It was open to an ornate illustration of a many limbed tree, curling about chaotically in whorls of neat black ink. Various names of elders, aristocracy and even some common folks were penned in.

"This is the bloodline of those that earn their Unveiling," he explained. "Most of the citizens will Unveil at one point or another. Many seeds are planted here, doctor, and the Almighty Ash will tell us when those seeds are ready to bloom forth. Some move faster than others. But then there are some...well, I'm sorry to say, good sir, that some seeds sprout weeds rather than bouquets. And I simply see no record of the Sanguire bloodline having obtained an Unveiling in the past. I'm sorry, doctor and although I'm grateful for what you've done for me and for the city, the ruling stands that it's just not meant to be."

Silas swallowed hard and studied the book. The High Lord wasn't lying. He could not see any trace of his ancestors located in the sprawling diagram. Before the book snapped shut with a cloud of dust, he noted a small illustration framing one corner of the page. A small white flower, encircled in a crimson root. An idea germinated in Silas's mind, much like the seed that the High Lord had spoken of. But this would be a growth that would nourish and bloom into something arcane and unheard of. He knew what to do, even as the High Lord rested a sympathetic hand on his shoulder.

"I'm sorry Silban, but some of us are just born better."

A maelstrom tore through his mind. So many thoughts, ideas, regrets, fears, emotions. They collided together in a haphazard storm that threatened to destroy the shroud that contained his very sanity. DeCinis was a bastard, a vile blood of an ingrate beast who couldn't even get his name right. Silas would show him. He had heard the stories about the flower of course, but he never dared to try. Why would he, when he would surely be Unveiling naturally and very soon? He'd assumed he would be the first of his bloodline to do so.

As he walked along the street, he reached up and tugged at his own face as though to prove a point to himself. The skin held tight and fast. No sign of sloughing or impending Unveiling. It wouldn't stay that way for long. He just needed some assistance.

Our Lady of Tears Cemetery loomed before him, a massive wrought iron gate surrounded by high stone walls. It was an imposing facade for a place of rest, but it didn't intimidate Silas. He pressed through the gate and beheld the site. The burial grounds were generally kept immaculate, at least depending on what breed of blood ran through your veins upon death. It was unfortunately all too easy to identify the marble busts and pristine headstones of the High Lord lines against the flat and weed infested grounds for those who perished still Veiled.

Silas pulled his coat tighter and shook a tuft of ash off his umbrella. He pressed onward, aiming towards a row of pristine marble mausoleums. The night was gentle, the ash drifting softly amidst the lantern light from the street. A soft breeze stirred up waves of gray, the lightest come-hither wisp of an age-old siren on a northern wind. It was the perfect night for the action at hand.

Silas ducked behind the mausoleum before him and inspected the back of the necropolis. It was there, as he expected, a gentle, alabaster bloom spiraling forth from the gray waste, encircled with the telltale crimson root system. The *Bloodroot* was easy pickings for a doctor trained in the ways of the green, and he plucked the plant with eagerness and glee. It held fast but with a bit of effort and a grunt of exertion, he managed to remove the plant. A soft thud echoed from the other side of the mausoleum wall, but he paid it no mind.

He grasped the flower and curled the long red root upon his hand, slipping it into his jacket pocket. As he made his way out of the cemetery, Silas took one last look behind him. The name *Anguis* was carved above the entry portal to the necropolis. Silas cursed under his breath, patted the flower within his pocket, and vowed that Delphine would never discover what he had done.

He confirmed it upon returning to his workshop. The *Bloodroot* grew only in the crypts and cemeteries where it intertwined with the dead. It was a symbiotic bloom that preserved the corpses and allowed them to maintain an aura of dignity, even as it fed upon what little remained of their vitality. In essence, the *Bloodroot* eternally embalmed its host body and to remove it would cause the body to crumble into dust, just another pile of ash amidst the eternal gray. Sacrifices had to be made, for what use did the dead have for everlasting beauty? Dead things were meant to rot.

Delphine came to call later that day, brushing ash off of her shoulder as she collapsed her umbrella and greeted her companion with a quick kiss on the cheek. Silas mentioned that he had work to do (conveniently omitting the nature of it and her ancestor's role in obtaining the ingredients) and she stole away to the rear garden to practice her marksmanship. Ashfall Hollow was known as a city of refinement, but there were darker dregs that lurked just beyond the fringe of society. One could never be too careful, and so Delphine Anguis often took it upon herself to secret a small, collapsible crossbow on her person should the need arise. She had never been one to comply with the societal expectations of a "proper lady", preferring to spend her day hunting in the woods on the outskirts of the city, fermenting her own wine from the essence obtained from her prey.

The prey-beasts themselves were easy creatures to bring down, gangly and awkward, with their ridiculous mops of hair and soft pink flesh. It was almost too easy, but occasionally she encountered one that took it upon itself to craft their own defense from crude rock and metal. She had taken a slash to the shoulder from a prey-beast on one particular hunt and had ended up in the healing arms of one Dr. Silas Sanguire. After patching her up, they had bonded over their mutual interest in studying the various natural phenomena around the city. She was more in tune with the wild beasts, while he focused on the plant life abound, and thus a connection was formed.

Silas reminisced these very thoughts to himself as he watched her fire one perfect shot after another at the wooden targets constructed in the garden. He knew he was lucky and surely a lady such as her deserved a man capable of a grand Unveiling. She was worth it. He'd show her that she was, if only she'd see him for the potential he was capable of.

As the dim sky above grew darker amidst the ash fall and the great star retreated further, he busied himself in his library and laboratory, consulting various texts to learn how best to harvest the *Bloodroot*. It didn't seem to be overly complicated. The consensus in his library presented multiple options to the good doctor.

Whenever Delphine would stop in to check on him, he would excuse himself for researching the *Graverot* moss for additional medicinal properties. They took a short break to chat over Lotuswort tea and fatcakes (unhealthy, but a rare indulgence made from the chewy subcutaneous harvests from the most recent crop of prey-beasts), and she eventually saw herself out the door.

"I'm proud of you, Silas," she said before departing. It was a comforting gesture and one he did appreciate, although cynicism gnawed at the back of his skull. Perhaps she was just placating him?

"And you as well, my dear," he replied and gave her a quick kiss before she returned to the gray swept shadows beyond his entry hall.

After he made certain that Delphine had departed, Silas drew the heavy velvet curtains across the window to his workshop and locked the door tight. The rest of the night was spent avoiding the specter of a restful sleep and busying himself with the various tools around his lab. The single sprig of *Bloodroot* he obtained had proven to be more bountiful than previously anticipated.

Through the course of the night, Dr. Silas Sanguire conducted multiple experiments in the shadows of his specimen cabinets. The enigmatic flower was brewed into a soup which he heartily devoured (adding just a dusting of cinnamon for flavor). After consuming the concoction, he leaned back in his red leather reclining chair and closed his eyes. Weariness overtook him briefly, but something stirred further within. He felt it swiftly grow, a wash of red, foaming, and opalescent within the shards of synaptic sparks that permeated his gray matter. There was something to this plant after all. Perhaps he had been a fool to ignore it all this time. And then, the red wave dissipated. It flowed back into the gentle sea of his subconscious, never to be dredged from the depths again. Unless he convinced it otherwise.

He had previously set aside a small helping of the pure white petals, which he decided to next consume raw. By candlelight, he recorded his experiences, the physical feelings, and intense emotions that the delicate properties of the plant imparted upon his physiology. The raw petals seemed to coat his tongue with a thin film. Silas found it irritating and swiftly tore through his small wine cabinet searching for something to quell the discomfort. Plenty of wine was consumed on this night, the fermented essence of the prey-beasts that Delphine had brought back the prior week. His head swam, thoughts percolating and swirling.

Within this haze, he conducted the next experiment, perhaps one he would not have attempted in a sober state of mind. Dr. Sanguire cut the crimson root into tiny chunks and boiled them in a beaker over a small, lit burner. The essence bubbled and foamed, catching sparks of candlelight before flickering out of existence like a dying star. Then he filled a sterilized syringe with the pinkish concoction, tied a rubber cord around his forearm, and injected the *Bloodroot* directly into his body.

Silas Sanguire had always heard the rumors that there existed a plant that could speed along or imbue the process of Unveiling. He believed he had discovered it. A momentous breakthrough, a scientific boon that the Ashen would empty their pockets to obtain. Silas would distribute it from his workshop, discreetly, if need be and would not only gain fame and wealth but would also help those who suffered from the malady of remaining Veiled.

"Some are born better," were the words spoken by the ungrateful High Lord. Silas was confident. Tomorrow night, at the ceremony. He'd accompany Delphine and he'd show them the light. He'd prove himself to be a brilliant mind and worthy of his companion. He just...needed to rest for now. But it was difficult. The red wave had returned, more ferocious than ever. A combination of the various means of imbibing the herb was unleashing a tempest within the good doctor. He felt it, he could smell it and taste it. And he wanted more. More beyond that which the wine in his cabinets could offer.

Oh, he would be seen. And heard. And he would dine and sup on Lords and Ladies while bathing in their admiration and sweeter spices still. He willed the red wave to subside to the best of his ability and knew that his time was swiftly at hand. But for now...for now he needed to...

"Wake up, you sleepy wretch!"

The red, the white, the grey. The wine, the flower, the ash. Everything and nothing. He was all a part of it. He reached up to his ears, ran his fingers along his skin seeking the seam that surely had to have developed overnight. It had to be there, it had to (they'd see him and hear him and it would be glorious, oh so glorious and—)

"Silas, we're going to be late! And you're not even dressed yet!"

He greeted the world with a rush of hot, tacky breath. Delphine recoiled with a grimace. Beyond the disgusted scowl, she looked radiant. The violet flecks in her eyes were accented with golden swirls painted on her face with arcane, ceremonial designs only meant for the most momentous of special occasions. Her dark hair was pulled up into a sensible bun, accompanied by threads of glowing red satin. Her usual simple black dress was filigreed with more interwoven strands of gold and red that seemed to dance gaily in the flickering candlelight. This luminous vision beyond the dancing flames brought him to full sobriety.

He wanted to caress her skin (but not harshly, she'd want to leave it intact for the ceremony) and thank her for everything. Silas pulled himself to his feet, smiled, then promptly rushed to the lavatory.

Delphine sighed impatiently and adjusted her face. The wet sound of spattering sick resounded from beyond the hastily closed door. She couldn't help but wonder what he had been up to all night. His normally tidy laboratory was a mess. Beakers and specimen jars were tipped over haphazardly and a tin pot nearby was coated with a sweet-smelling white film. She recoiled in disgust for the third time since entering her companion's workshop and, for the first time in a good while, began to have second thoughts.

But then, Silas was a good man if somewhat irascible and occasionally insecure, although this latter mindset was unwarranted. He was handsome, aging gracefully and an intelligent individual. She knew his insecurities were only further inflamed from his lack of Unveiling but in time, he would grow out of it. All of the Ashen did sooner or later. Didn't they?

Silas returned from the lavatory, brushing a shaking hand across his mustache. He looked at once older and more youthful, with a strange sheen coating his curiously sagging skin. He smacked his lips, turned away from the woman and pulled a set of dress clothes out of his wardrobe.

"Give me just a few minutes?" he requested quietly.

Delphine nodded, a crease of concern crossing her luminous visage. She turned toward the covered front window of her companion's workshop and pulled it aside, gazing out at the street beyond. It was a quiet night, for most of the town would be gathered at DeCinis's estate. She would join them in merriment soon enough, but quiet streets often bred the most opportunities for confrontation as well. She checked her sleeve and felt comfort at the rigid shape hidden within, brushing her forearm with authority and confidence.

A moment later, Silas returned dressed in a smart, pressed brown shirt, overcoat, and tricorn hat. It was an outfit that would not draw attention to himself but still commanded an aura of sophistication. He snuffed out the candle on his worktable and took her hand in his.

"Let us have a very memorable evening," he said, as the companions embraced in the still quiet of the night.

The rattling of the coach wheels on the ash laden cobblestone evoked a symphony of pain in Silas's head. He clutched it and stared out the gilded window at the passing architecture. Obsidian spires reached high to touch a rose-tinted sky, the faintest blush of a forgotten golden star struggling in vain to peer beyond the suffocating gray veil. The ominous spires and peaked arches indicated they had arrived in the part of Ashfall Hollow that was more well-to-do than the Withered packed dregs that played host to Silas's workshop and lab. He sighed as he watched the wisp of his old life drift away into the swirling shade. Then he ran a hand across his face, felt the encroaching seams beneath his skin, and smiled a secret grin.

A soft, cold hand touched his and intertwined with his fingers.

"No matter what, you're an important man to me," Delphine assured him.

He turned to grin at her and yet, in the back of his mind, the red wave whispered and told him that she was simply placating him. What would a woman like her want with a man who could not Unveil without artificial assistance? No, he had more to offer. He just had to prove it. He'd show them all the light. His opportunity had arrived at the cessation of wheels on stone and the creaking of an opening door. DeCinis Manor loomed overhead. Silas disembarked, helped his companion down from the carriage and straightened his coat. Right then. On with the show.

A random Withered answered the heavy oak door as Blair was preoccupied with directing the rest of the servants about the hall. The sunken gray things scurried about, rasping as they delivered hors d'oeurves to the attendees. Beyond the smattering of Withered, the hall was a grand sight to behold. Candlelight danced behind glass bulbs

and sconces, illuminating bunting of red, gold, and black the traditional colors of the Unveiling ceremony). Various townsfolk mingled
and chatted. A musical lilt of laughter here, a wet sucking of sodden
flesh there, all imposed upon a great velvet, maroon colored rug that
stretched the length of the hall. A gentle strain of violins echoed from a
far-flung corner providing a regal and slightly morose ambiance to the
proceedings.

"This is phenomenal," Delphine whispered in awe. She grasped
Silas's arm with a smile, leading him further into the hall. He glimpsed
the folds emerging on her own face and grinned, reveling in what await-
ed their future.

"We heard the news, or rather the lack thereof," came a high-
pitched voice. Delphine and Silas turned as one. She broke into a wide
grin and he into a frown at the sight of the twins.

Hall & Skati were distant relatives of the Anguis family and thus
connected to Delphine through a thin line of familial blood. The pair
were short in stature and sharp featured, a pair of war pikes made flesh
and sporting the same ability to cut deep. They gazed up at the pair in
unison, presenting their hooked noses and cheekbones sharp enough
to carve a prey-beast. Both were practically hanging on by a thread and
at first glance, Silas wasn't sure they'd be able to maintain their composure until the Grand Unveiling. They were dressed in identical fashion,
unisex black slacks, buckled shoes and veiled headdresses filigreed with
gold strands.

"Lovely to see you here, Delphine," Hall, the twin on the left, said.

"And unexpected for your physician friend to make it through
the door," Skati concluded.

Silas took a deep breath and forced a smile. The red wave com-
pelled him to. Keep composure. Soon all will be well. All will see the
light, burn as it may.

"Well, I have been holding back on the fatcakes, so I was able to slip through the threshold quite easily, thank you," he quipped.

The twins scoffed and Delphine giggled. "I'll have you know," she said, "that Silas is here of his own accord to support my Unveiling tonight. I have no doubt I'll be doing the same for him next year as well."

"Time will tell," Hall stated.

"Until then, enjoy yourselves. Or at least, make a sincere effort to," Skati said. The pair bowed in unison and turned away to mingle further into the hall.

Silas groaned.

"I know, I know," Delphine patted his arm assuredly.

"It's just... they're so small. All I need is one clenched fist to deck the pair of them," he said. "Could I? Do you think? I could do so with utmost stealth and satisfaction..."

"Yes, you could," Delphine said, raising a tapered finger. "But you won't." She dropped the finger down and then brushed it gently on his face. She frowned as part of his skin bunched around her nail, as though sagging.

"Ah, the lovely Miss Anguis and my favorite foot tender, together in one joyous happenstance." A velvety voice caught their attention. Silas frowned as DeCinis approached the pair with a flourish of his satin cape.

The good doctor groaned as a sudden streak of hunger shot through his midsection. They hadn't even made it five meters into the hall without being accosted by minglers. He glanced wistfully off to the side at a banquet table piled with sumptuous strips of meat, fatcakes, and a sparkling, cascading fountain of wine. No, it wasn't hunger. It was thirst. Were those...white petals floating in the wine? Surely, they wouldn't...? No, nothing there. Nothing except endless red, gently sloshing about in fine crystal goblets, begging for release. To be washed away in a frenzy of gnashing teeth and greedy lips.

"- imported from the farthest reaches beyond Maldaka. I believe sourced from the silica cliffs that the region is so famous for. It's beautiful, wouldn't you agree?" DeCinis had been speaking the whole time.

"Very beautiful," Silas agreed. "How does it taste?"

Delphine and the High Lord both cocked confused eyebrows. "Taste?" DeCinis asked. "My good man, I generally attempt to avoid consuming my own glassware. An interesting palate you have...and uh, you as well, Lady Anguis. If you'll excuse me."

He glanced toward the back of the room in the direction of a grand marble staircase. The High Lord falsified a cry of recognition as an excuse to steal away.

"What was that?" Delphine asked, her face etched with a glaze of concern and a hint of irritation. "I'd ask you to please not eat the wine glasses or table settings."

"I do not--" Silas shook his head. The red was there still, ever present and always swirling about. Each shake of his head further frenzied the storm as it slowly eroded the veneer that was holding his flesh together. "While don't we dance? Yes? Yes, come, let us dance."

It was a fine idea in retrospect. He and Delphine whiled away the hazy, golden night in twirls, dips, and elaborate gestures as they swayed to the delicate string music. It was a nice moment, a boost of serotonin that offered to penetrate the ever-growing storm in the back of his mind. Yet, as she caressed his face, Silas felt it beginning to slough away even further. He was ready to unmask, to discard his own identity and reveal his true self.

She herself experienced the slow detachment of her former identity but this was to be expected at an Unveiling. His was not meant to be. Silas Sanguire was meant to hover on the edge of "proper" society, to cling tenuously to the shadows that lurked beyond the gilded halls and crystal goblets. He should not have been here on this night.

The *Bloodroot* had worked. He acknowledged this even as he dipped Delphine low and inhaled a wisp of her floral perfume. A delicate scent, touched by death's embrace. He had desecrated a corpse and experimented upon his own body and mind. Yet it hadn't quelled the quiet storm. It had enhanced it, unleashed something red and wild, locked behind a forbidden door of insecurity, the latch dissolved by the chemicals flowing through his brain. He regretted his actions and yet, he reveled in the red yet to come. A red that he would unleash on all those who had wronged him. The storm told him that it would steer him on course towards that ever-begotten golden light lurking behind the eternal grey.

The time was now.

The violins came to an abrupt silence and the clinking of glass echoed throughout the room. All ceased their actions and turned towards the apex of the room. Hall and Skati stood a few feet from Delphine and Silas, smug smirks plastered on their drooping faces. Around him, Silas could see those who would Unveil sporting the tell-tale sagging flesh and strands of sallow skin ready to be removed.

Harold DeCinis appeared with a ceremonial glass in hand. The golden goblet he held was inlaid with shards of onyx and rubies. It gleamed under the candlelight, as did the High Lord's ever-present grin. He held the goblet aloft and beckoned for his attendees to do the same with their own glasses.

"Tonight, like many nights before and still to come, is an important one. To you, good citizens of our fair city, a momentous occurrence is at hand. For centuries, we have labored under the pall of the sacred Ash, graciously imparted by our forefathers to obscure the golden star above that would threaten to destroy our very flesh."

A chorus of boos and hisses rang throughout the hall.

DeCinis continued. "Tonight, we celebrate the Unveiling, the time upon which our most special and accomplished members of society can shed their veneer and reveal their true selves to the world to strike fear into the slight souls of the prey-beasts. And for those of you not chosen, well, we welcome your support."

He chuckled derisively and Silas swore he saw the High Lord glance in his direction.

"Tonight, my people, we take off our masks to show our superiority and what truly dwells beneath this festering skin! I raise a toast of wine, culled fresh from the latest hunt to the Ash, to the Hollow and to OUR TRUE SELVES! You may now Unveil!"

A raucous cry of exaltation spread among the revelers. Glasses were raised and dunked back sloppily, wine spilling about haphazardly onto the gilded floor. No matter, the Withered would clean it up after the festivities. Delphine linked her arm with Silas as the good doctor looked first to the twins, to Blair the butler, and then to the High Lord. Of course, a man of DeCinis's stature would have Unveiled years prior. The skin he had been wearing was simply ceremonial, to show the rabble that he was "one of them." Silas did not fall for the ruse. He was prepared to show them all that he was the superior one. He was ready to be seen, to be heard, and all it took was one good pull.

Delphine beamed at her companion as she reached up to her sagging face. The rest of the chosen followed suit. The hall was awash in sounds that some might find appalling, others might find rapturous. There was the slicing of skin, the wet tear of flesh from muscle, gargled gasps as those Unveiling breathed into a new life. The licking of fleshless lips, sighs of satisfaction, and cries of unbridled, blighted ecstasy.

He looked to her, his beautiful Delphine as she Unveiled. Her facial skin peeled off in wet strands, revealing the raw muscle beneath. In time, this would become encased in a thin membrane of filmy, white sheen, a porcelain doll with the heart of a voracious predator. Her fangs unfurled from the thin sac in her palate where all the Ashen held them until the night of ceremony. Her hair fell off in ragged clumps and Silas had no doubt that she would collect it before leaving and dress it upon a mannequin head as remembrance to her former life. Her beautiful gold flecked eyes flitted in the candlelight to become one with the flame, an effervescent red that shone with vitality.

The Unveiled lit up the hall with great cries and animalistic hisses that would be heard throughout the Hollow and the forests to the north. The prey-beasts would huddle in fear and whisper among themselves about the cruel hunts to come. But on this night, there was celebration to be had. The Unveiled hurled the remnants of their former lives into the air. The high ceilings of the grand hall was awash in a rainfall of flesh. Dancing light glimpsed swiftly between hollowed out eyes and mouths, old flesh given way to new and thrown skyward towards the damnable golden star in a vast display of rebellion and symbolism of life born anew.

Tears ran salted tracks down Delphine's raw musculature as she licked at the air and flexed her new fangs. Silas was proud of her and all that she had accomplished. He knew that she would be proud of him. She turned toward him, eyes aglow.

"I've Unveiled, darling. I'm ready. What do you think?"

"I see you and you're ravishing," he said. "Now, I want you and everyone here, to see me."

Silas Sanguire, the doctor and purveyor of rare botanical specimens of Ashfall Hollow proceeded to Unveil. He reached up and grasped his flesh. He pulled his face downwards. It did not go smoothly. His own Unveiling had been imparted upon through artificial means and thus was a phenomenon quite unnatural. Silas could hear the chuckles around him, undoubtedly laughing at what they perceived was a vain attempt to show he belonged.

He did belong. He knew it. He just needed to try a little harder. The rest of his face came loose with one ragged, unseemly tear and he cried out into the grey and golden night. It was not a cry of ecstasy and pride, rather a shriek of anger and pain as the red wave evolved into an unbridled tempest.

"Silas, what—" The newly Unveiled Delphine stepped back, the bottom of her dress squelching upon the discarded face of another attendee. Gasps and whispers spread throughout the hall. The twins stepped forward cautiously to observe.

"I've Unveiled too," he whispered in a wet, pained gasp. "Look at me! Delphine, you don't need to be ashamed. None of you do!" Silas spun around and pointed at the throng. One fang unfurled, the other caught inside an undeveloped sac. Ragged clumps clung to his musculature, the result of an Unveiling that was not meant to be.

"What is the meaning of this?" DeCinis stepped forward. He had removed his own ceremonial mask, revealing the smooth white veneer and crimson eyes beneath. "Dr. Sanguire, I know for a fact that you're - that you're…" He seemed too perplexed to continue.

"Most peculiar," Hall said.

"And intriguing. Yet hideous," Skati finished.

Silas tapped his glistening visage with his finger. "I found the secret. Some are born better, so it has been said. But perhaps we no longer need to adhere to who is chosen and who is left behind. All it takes is a little bit of science, a bit of experimentation. I can set us all free, every citizen can be Unveiled!"

"Blasphemy!" DeCinis roared.

"No, truth," Silas said, relishing the feeling of his new face. "I used-" He paused, catching his breath in great hitches. He felt the rage, the storm boiling further. "I used the *Bloodroot* culled from the cemetery. It's all we need! Delphine, the bloom came from your family plot! Don't you see?! It means that you and I, we are one, now and always. Your bloodline helped make this happen!"

Delphine stepped back. She felt the rigid object hidden in her sleeve and slipped it downward to her hand. Her moment, her revelation, her rebirth. It had been overshadowed by the man she trusted and loved, a man who had…who had…

"Desecrated!" Delphine cried out, tears streaming. "You vandalized my family to become an...abomination. Silas, this is not how it works. You cannot- you cannot urge this on through experimentation. No, this happens naturally. In time...and yet..."

She trailed off, heart shattered, and soul torn asunder. This wasn't how this night was supposed to happen. The rest of the Unveiled and their own companions began to inch nervously toward the exit, whispers and gossip rippling through the masses like a wave. A wave that was beginning to crescendo into something -

"Pathetic," Hall said.

"Pathetic," Skati agreed.

"Yes, pathetic," DeCinis echoed.

"Pathetic," Blair said from the shadows.

Silas turned toward Delphine. He held out a hand to her, urging her to take it. She shrunk away and nodded silently in agreement with the assessment. The fact that her words were unspoken was all Silas Sanguire could take. He closed his eyes and flexed his one fang. He surrendered to the wave, to the storm. How could one little flower have imparted such rage, such bloodlust? He felt the chemicals flowing in his veins, the petals and broth percolating in his stomach. He felt the delicate bloom give way to the red, washed away in a tidal onslaught of fury. He needed--

The storm spoke again and told him what it needed to instill calm. It needed blood.

Silas spun around and lashed out towards Hall and Skati. Pure rage and insanity fueled his strength and both the twins fell in one powerful strike. Their essence stained the floor, pooling among the discarded wastes of skin. The throng squealed like prey-beasts as they stampeded toward the exit.

Silas ducked low beneath a table and pooled fresh rivulets of blood from the slain twins into his mouth. It was divine, a shock to the system. And yet the storm inside him became even more powerful. Red flakes rained from the sky within his mind. The storm had lied to him, it had only grown more powerful. As the former doctor turned toward High Lord DeCinis, he realized that the flakes falling from his own personal storm was not blood, but red-tinged ash. It all made sense now. He needed to coat the ash with blood, turn the gray into red and then, only then, would he become known and accepted. No, acceptance was for the weak willed. He would become FEARED.

Silas continued his onslaught and grappled at the High Lord. The aristocrat fought back; physical strength allotted him but an extra moment of life. Yet Silas pushed forward, fueled by the red waste within and sank his single, half-developed fang into the throat of the man who thought himself to be his better.

"Born better, aged better, like a fine wine," Silas whispered as he pulled DeCinis's body to the floor. How ironic, he thought, to forever stain the very floor he treaded upon during his life of luxury, lording above to all those below. No longer.

Silas wiped his mouth, his raw musculature burning with adrenaline. He smoothed back his hair and half of it tumbled off, catching his collar, and hanging limply like a dead animal. Delphine stood among four corpses and rivers of blood. He couldn't recall slaying Blair, which was a shame; he'd have liked to have savored that.

Silas took a step towards his companion, his lover, fresh blood sparkling off of his half-Unveiled face. He squelched in the rivers at his feet, red rainfall from the storm. Sloughed off faces lie scattered about like party favors, their previous owners having had no time to revel in their discarding. No matter. Nothing mattered except for the Unveiled woman before him.

Silas stepped forward again and spread his hands wide. "One more dance, my dear? One more dance, my flower?" he asked.

Delphine shook her head and raised her hand. The collapsible crossbow was primed, cocked, and ready. "No more," she whispered and let loose a single bolt.

The storm was silenced. Silas felt the pierce of a wrought iron bolt and the gilded floor rushing to meet him. As the red receded and the grey took its place again, he reached out feebly to grasp his own discarded face. He pressed it weakly against the Unveiled flesh and it slipped back off into the collection of gore. He heard screaming in the haze that greeted his vision. It was the woman, the poisonous flower that had silenced the storm once and for all. Why was she screaming? There was no reason for such cacophony. Everything was right. He rolled over and gazed at a single flickering candle ensconced on the wall. No, it was the golden star. The sun. He had heard tales of how it had pierced the sky in the days before the Ashen had laid waste to the world. Before they had driven the prey-beasts back into the wild and reclaimed the cities for their own. Before the forefathers had released the weapons into the sky to bring about the eternal Ash.

Silas Sanguire had been seen. He had been heard. The sun had been Unveiled only for him, even as it and his life force dimmed from existence. He had seen the light and it was beautiful.

The Cannibal and The Barber
Spyder Collins

Candles twinkled about the operating theater. The flames, normally faint, flashed deep and bright like dying stars. They provided a dim dash of light, creating creeping shadows about the walls. Natural light labored to break through the ceiling windows of the southeast facing theater, already dimmed by the low hanging clouds of an autumn morning. Never mind the tint from the chemicals and the human exhaust of the theater. Even on the brightest summer mornings light was scarce, but on days such as these, the candles were the only thing that reduced the eye strain of the doctors and their gore-riddled tasks. The rest of the building was brick masonry painted a bright white to aid in reflective light, and difficult to uphold.

The theater keeper, Anne Booth-Carter, was set off to the side, obscured by shadow. So much that she was barely visible. Anne scanned the theater. She had prepared it in such a manner that would impress even the most pretentious of doctors. But as it was, no one bothered to acknowledge its condition, let alone her presence. By all accounts,

Anne was invisible. Most days this suited her. Would it be so difficult for someone to once appreciate her work? she wondered.

But far be it for her to bother. She tended to the excrement, piss, spit, and snot with as much satisfaction as the residual blood, visceral, and limbs. She was disappointed by the amount of blood the linens had slacked up, before they were tossed aside for her to tend to, and by the sawdust that sopped up most of the blood into marbles. Still, it was more than she could have asked for, the residual carnage of a messy theater that no one else paid any mind to.

The gentle tones of a flutist, Andrew, drew back her attention. He serenaded the patrons beneath the sounds of male attendants and the murmuring of onlookers. A crowded room of scholars and doctors had gathered to witness a parade of surgeries. They all ignored Andrew and his sweet melody. They gawked, took notes, and chattered amongst themselves. Unmindful of his musical prowess, all except Anne. She admired the simple things.

The doctors prepared themselves for surgery, their blood-stained aprons draped over their equally blighted surgical gowns. Anne found it amusing the blood that flowed through the theater made its way onto their clothing more than the sawdust covered floor. But how she loved the theatrics, the visuals, the sounds that echoed about the theater, all the while the tunes from Andrew's flute carried a soft undertone.

She settled back, unseen, and prepared. And so it began, the screams, the flow of blood, the death, and the whines of survivors. An afternoon of surgical miracles and failures.

The sounds of the flute faded, and Anne closed her eyes, taking in the sound of despair and death. A whimsical smile spread her lips.

⁂

"There's more blood than usual, it appears," Doctor Godwin remarked.

Anne kept her head down, untucking her tresses so they would fall over her face and conceal her uneasiness.

Doctor Grover Godwin Esquire. Even his name was unsightly to Anne. By all accounts, he was the catch of London. Tall, stately, muscular, with a firm chin covered by a peppered goatee below shockingly blue eyes. Educated, of course, well-spoken, and he had a dashing smile of perfect teeth. Yes, he was attractive (even she would admit), wealthy, and prone to charity, as shown by his willingness to work in Whitechapel. But one only needed to remember he was married with a child and spent his time away from the surgical table chasing bloomers that did not belong to him.

She spied him eyeing her, as he'd come to do. Anne's frame was more so than the average woman, tall and well filled-out. She felt his eyes following her curves as she moved through the theater, ignoring him.

One would think she would take reward for her fetching beauty, working around esteemed doctors and scholars and all. At least that was the talk about the operating theater. But she was an odd beauty who would rather live in the filth of London's East End in a small hovel in Whitechapel.

Doctor Godwin was quick to give up his scrutinizing gaze, much to Anne's relief.

"Very well, on with it then." She heard him concede.

Anne peered through the hair that still covered her face. She spied a stain of blood on his wire framed spectacles.

She recalled when her interest in blood was first piqued. It was after she began menstruating, when her grandmother proclaimed her entrance into womanhood, while her mother proclaimed whore-dom. The blood, the almost tar that rested in her rags fascinated her. Even the smell she found intriguing. It was at an early age that she explored it with her fingers, eventually putting it into her mouth.

It didn't seem odd to her to play with her blood as she did. By her grandmother's reaction to the cleaning, it was not a pleasant thing. But for Anne, it was a point of interest, which made her job at the theater that much more enjoyable. In fact, Anne often collected her menstrual blood in mason jars. She hid them beneath her bed to explore on off times, when chores, beatings and loneliness allowed her.

"Such a deathly stare, for such a fetching woman," Doctor Godwin commented, interrupting her thoughts.

Anne remained silent. She watched patiently as the Doctor exited.

"Daft and pompous," she exhaled.

Anne talked to no one unless it was necessary. She held long and detailed conversations with herself, however. She tucked her hair behind her ears and, with her face lit with excitement, she panned about the operating theater. Indeed, it had been a messy and fruitful day of surgeries, which increased her pickings and pleased her palate, as well.

"Let's begin, Anne." She rubbed her gloves together and grabbed her supplies.

She started with the walls, wiping down the occasional blood that somehow made its way onto the walls. Next, she walked to the viewing area to ensure the chairs were lined-up in an orderly fashion. She would also look for notebooks, coats, or hats and place them in the foyer for patrons that left them. Every so often she would find things of value, but unless it was a coin, she always placed in the foyer.

She completed the viewing area, then went to the floors surrounding the surgical table. She scooped up the clumps of saw dust and placed them in a bin for washing and reuse. She swept the circumference of the room and smiled. "You're making great time and the reward will be well worth it."

She turned her attention to the surgical table and the baskets below. "What have we here?"

She pulled out two wicker baskets. She opened the first, and there among the blood-soaked sawdust was a hearty arm, hand, and foot. In the other basket, a liver, and a kidney.

Removing the organs from the second basket, Anne placed them atop the surgical table and proceeded to prep them. She rubbed them vigorously, loosening the top layer of the organ. Then with a surgeon's care, she sliced, first the liver, followed by the kidney into comfortable portions. Then she returned the sliced organ into the wicker basket.

"A feast for a queen, Queen Anne," she chuckled.

She moved to the basin. Removing her catch from the basket, she placed them in the basin. She let the sliced organs soak in water, while she gathered the baskets and moved to the lower level to burn them in the incinerator. She carried both baskets by the handle, one in each hand, making her way down the stairs to the lower level. Maneuvering down the staircase, baskets in tow, she felt a spring in her step. She felt chipper this eve, but why she was uncertain.

She stood before the encased pyre. "The aroma of burning blood and the cackle of the flames - how they calm the soul," she remarked, tossing the less savory body parts into the fire, one at a time.

Anne headed back to the operating theater, a spark of enthusiasm as she finished her chores. She took linen from the station and then to the basin. She removed the contents from the basin and patted them dry, wrapped them and placed them in her bag. Anne did one final sweep, ensuring every corner, crack and crevice had been reviewed for anything of value and to remove any unsightly remnants.

Then Anne was off, bag in hand. Everything was as she pleased.

The early morning air was crisp. The smell of rubbish wafted from what decent air there was to breathe. She took a moment to raise the collar of her jacket before setting down the street. Her pinet boots clicked rhythmically along the cobblestone. Her pace wasn't hastened, as one might expect a woman's to be in the early morning among the vagrants and drunks in the gutters. Anne could care less; she saw past all that. Rather, she concentrated on the radiant glow of the lamp light. It reminded her of the sun rising above the pasture back home in Dorsett. Or how the mist layered the cobblestone in a wet sheen that lit beneath the light of the gas lamp. The sound of the neighing horses and the rattle of the occasional carriage that happened by, even at this hour. The city had much to take in with each walk home and into work, but more now, when most of the city slept.

The dark alleyways sparked glowing cigarettes and the moans of addicts. She passed countless along her path. Whitechapel was the armpit of London, without question. The brothels, pubs and opium dens were at every look. "Best watch out, lassie," a vagrant from the gutter along her path warned. "The Ripper roams these streets."

Anne ignored him. She didn't bother to quicken her pace. She did, however, turn her head. Even from a distance, she could smell the stale liquor and smoke on his breath.

She lived close to the theater, which worked perfect for her with her hours and penchant to daydream. Home was a small hovel past a network of alleyways along a straight stretch of cobblestone street. She glanced from time to time towards the other flats she passed on the way to hers. Most were drowned in darkness but on occasion, she'd spy a candle burning in a frightened child's room or in the bedroom of lovers.

As she approached her flat, she crossed paths with her neighbor, Mr. Kosminski. He was a quiet man, kind and respectful, though odd. Barber by trade, he kept very strange hours, so she didn't think to question why he was returning home with his bag at such an hour. Anne had her own life to tend to.

"Good morning, miss," Mr. Kosminski offered a tip of his hat.

"Good morning, sir," Anne replied. Charming, she thought, as the two headed towards their building. She noted his bag looked more medical then perhaps a barber's bag, and swore she saw a tuft of hair stained in blood but was difficult to see under lamplight.

She thought nothing more of it as Mr. Kosminski switched hands to place the bag behind him, offering her the lead down the path with an open hand.

Their stroll was short and quiet. Neither talked, though the barber showed a touch of interest from time to time. When they reached the front door, he held it open for her.

"Hope the lady enjoys her evening," he commented as he opened the door to his flat.

Anne lowered her head shyly and opened her door. She felt his eyes on her, not as a neighbor but as a man. And truth be told, it felt good.

"And the same to the gentleman," she returned as she closed the door. She locked it and swooned just a bit before removing her bonnet. It found its way to the floor beside the door as did her boots. In her stocking feet, she rushed to her icebox to maintain the freshness of her catch. She left out a kidney atop her cooking counter. It was small, a child's perhaps, or one malformed to warrant surgical removal. She stoked the stove, lighting the wood already placed. She made sure there was a good flame and took to the kidney. She ground the fillets in the chopper with slow and steady turns to get the consistency she liked. The freshness was more than apparent as bubbles of blood exited the grinder with lean strands of meat. Once complete, she placed the grinded organ into a cast iron pan and set it atop the stove. She took a small piece from the pan, working it around in her mouth before chewing and swallowing it. She took two eggs from the refrigerator and cracked them open into the cast iron pan.

The rich aroma of her meal filled her senses. Even Mr. Kosminski made comments about the delicious smells that floated into his flat. Anne had toyed with the idea of having him over one of the times the two crossed paths. Perhaps she would, if she could only gather the nerve. He seemed the type to understand her, odd, like her.

Anne pulled her meal from the stovetop and slipped it onto a waiting plate. She sat at her small dining table. Big enough for two, she thought with a smile. The scent of her meal was rich. Kidney let off an especially strong meaty scent and the fresh blood that stained the eggs a black tint raised her anticipation. As she spooned in a mouthful of egg and kidney, she dabbed the sides of her lips, and her smile spread at the flavor of it all.

She never ate well as a child. Even on a farm, her family was poor. Her father died when she was still young and her mother was unable to maintain the land, so it simply remained green from the healthy rain but never yielded much of anything edible. And what it did, mother kept for herself. Anne scrounged what she could and ate whatever her grandmother could bring her. Protein came from rats and the other vermin she was able to catch and kill. She grew to love the taste of raw rat, especially the bloody organs. She ate their hair and all.

After her meal, Anne cleaned up and put the wet dishes on a drainboard before retiring to her bedroom. The smell of egg and kidney had filled her bedroom, and she was quite pleased by it. As she dressed, her thoughts floated to Doctor Godwin and she could not help but feel disgusted. That intrusive look of wanting and eagerness for her to give in to his wealth and position. She had no interest in men with such feelings of entitlement.

Perhaps that was why she felt an attraction to Mr. Kosminski. He was humble, shy even, much like her. Mr. Kosminski, she thought with a giggle. She went to her mirror, peering at her reflection as she ran a brush through her acorn-colored hair.

Once it reached a suitable sheen, she set the hairbrush down and reached for a small jar set off to the side. It was a special jar, one her grandmother had given her. It was said to have special powers, the dark glass protected by a dragon whose tail wrapped around the glass with its tip jutting out about an inch, to lay across whatever surface it sat on. Its head was above the lip of the opening, which was hinged at the dragon's neck. It was lovely and ominous and perfect for its contents, but magical, not in the least.

Anne went to her work bag and returned with a small vial of blood she'd collected at the theater and some tonic water. She poured both into the jar, closed the lid, and shook it. A moment later, she set it down and reopened the dragon wrapped jar and dipped two fingers inside. She then placed her crimson finger onto her face and massaged the contents into her skin. She did this until she covered her entire face with fresh blood and tonic water. She placed a dab inside each nostril to draw the smell deep into her. Her fondness for blood was irrefutable.

Satisfied, she closed the lid to the jar and sucked the remnants from her finger until they were clean. She dried them on her gown and retired to bed, opening the anatomy book that was sitting on her nightstand.

The next afternoon, Anne woke and went about her day as normal. Chores, cleaning, and a spot of sitting by her front window watching the people of Whitechapel stroll by. It was what she medicated her brain with, the people of Whitechapel, people she didn't want to know, speak to, or even run into. But she did enjoy watching them, the more well-to-do and the vagrants that sauntered or stumbled by her window. Dare they look at her, though. She'd draw the drapes or turn her attention to her feet until she felt their gaze no more.

As she sat, she reminded herself that she required eggs for her meal this evening, liver perhaps, or something else that caught her palate at the theater. She grabbed her bag and set off to the general store.

As Anne departed the building, she felt the chill of the autumn air, inviting and fresh against her face. The early morning's cleansing had been delightful. Her face felt radiant after the blood mask. The cool air was just what her skin needed.

Collar up and head down, she headed east towards the general store. Her rhythmic steps were soon drowned by the clatter of horse-and-carriage and people talking on the street. Her route would take her passed Mr. Kosminski's barbershop, earning perhaps a smile and wave, if he noticed. The prospect of it made her smile.

The cobblestone still carried the moisture of the night's mist, but not the shimmer. The overcast skies deadened any glow. It amplified the noise of the town and dampened Anne's mood. She quickened her pace until she reached the row of shops where Mr. Kosminski's barber shop sat.

She crossed the street, dodging puddles and carriages. When she reached the other side, she righted herself. Straightening out her dress and checking her bonnet, she walked proper, just a bit slower than her normal pace. As she passed each shop, she peered at what reflection of herself she could see in the spare windows. When she reached the barbershop, a surprised expression met her gaze. Mr. Kosminski stood at the window of his shop. He had no customers and seemed bored.

Immediately, they were caught in one another's eyes. He was noticeably excited to see her, his eyes widened and brow raised. She, however, was embarrassed, and she tucked her head down and continued to walk.

A moment later, she heard, "Miss?"

Her breath caught in her throat. She slowed but did not stop, nor did she turn to acknowledge him.

"Miss, from Everly Flats? Neighbor?"

Anne had no choice but to stop. She turned to Mr. Kosminski and replied politely, "Yes, sir. You are my neighbor, Mr. Kosminski."

"Yes!" he replied with unnatural glee.

He had been so reserved, it was nice to see him like this. Gazing at him, she felt the butterflies. "I was just on my way to the market for some eggs." At that moment, Anne thought how dreadful to tell him such detail.

"I don't mean to detain you, miss." He paused for a moment, thoughtful. "May I ask your name?"

She smiled, and shyly lowered her eyes.

"If it's too much, I understand. We barely know each other."

"No," she replied. "Anne. Anne Booth-Carter."

"Miss Booth-Carter," he said with a dip of his head. He had her attention previously, but even more so now.

"Please, call me Anne."

"Anne, charmed. My name is Aaron Kosminski, and would be honored if you would call me Aaron." His accent was unusual, but it added a bit of mystery to him.

"Aaron, it is wonderful to put a name to you" Anne offered a short curtsey and a brighter smile than she had ever shown since perhaps her youth.

"I wanted to comment on the tantalizing aroma from your flat last night."

Anne smiled and lowered her eyes. "Dinner," she murmured. Without a thought, she continued, "Would you care to join me this evening?"

The worry on her face must have been evident.

"Are you sure?" he replied. "I don't want to intrude."

"No, not at all and yes, yes I am serious." Her expression softened.

"I would like that." He smiled. "What time shall I call?"

"We can meet along the path to our building after work."

"Perfect." Aaron looked into his shop. A patron had wandered in during their conversation. "See you tonight?"

"Tonight," she echoed.

Anne watched Aaron make his way into his shop to greet his customer. Worry gripped her. What would she make, would he like it, what if he doesn't like her once they sit down to a meal? She fretted all the way to the general store and back to her flat.

The late afternoon session had already begun when Anne arrived. She was late, very unlike her. She snuck to her spot along the back wall of the theater, gathering an annoyed glare from Doctor Godwin. She buried herself in the darkness to hide from any other angry eyes.

She took in Andrew's gentle play and drawing deep breaths of spoiled air. Soon, she thought, the theater would be hers. The next patient entered, for she had missed the entire first operation. If she recalled, it was a simple procedure to remove a gangrene finger. She stood by as the patient objected to the condition of the theater, which raised Anne's ire. If asked, she would challenge anyone to find a theater kept better. She was the only attendant that she knew of who stood, waiting to be called on to provide removal or cleaning of the area between surgeries, as needed. Which, honestly, seldom happened.

Anne closed her eyes. The sound of splitting flesh and pain serenaded her. If only for a while, she could sink into the pain of others and enjoy the waft of blood that passed her nose. It was why she was here, this and her appetite. The blood, gore, and suffering, it all brought her peace. It was intoxicating and she drifted.

The voice of Doctor Goodwin snapped her back. She opened her eyes to see the crowd of onlookers move out of the theater. Some held tears, others their stomachs, and many more were unaffected by the afternoon activities. Doctor Godwin thanked them all and accompanied them out of the theater. It was customary, so he could boast of his prowess in the theater or flirt with the wives of other junior surgeons observing.

Anne emerged as the last of the patrons left and Andrew put his flute up and exited. She donned her gown and gloves, and prayed Doctor Godwin would not return to the theater for a visit, or worse, a lecture.

She moved about the theater with thoughts of dinner with Aaron. She had to refrain from checking the baskets until she was certain all had left, and she was alone. It was quiet and Anne was making time until she heard a voice.

"Seems someone is in a hurry. Do we have a date?" Doctor Godwin's voice carried a light jest to it.

She ignored him and continued with her duties.

"Come on, at least acknowledge me." His plea sounded like a schoolboy's.

Anne sighed before she turned his way. "What can I do for you, Doctor?"

"Ah, your face. Nice to see it not covered by your hair."

Anne winced. In her haste, she had forgotten to remove her bonnet and lower her hair. "I have work to do. I do not disturb you while you work."

"Oh, but you do. On this very day, did you not wander into my theater late?" His tone darkened.

Anne moved over to the operating table, pushing the instruments aside and gathering the soiled linens. "Indeed, you are correct, and I do apologize."

"You know, I could have you removed," he remarked.

Anne's brow furrowed, "For one infraction?"

Doctor Godwin approached her.

Anne recoiled against the operating table. He was close, too close for her comfort.

"Yes," he replied, "and mind the way you speak to me." He tapped his finger on his chin and continued, "Or, we could make an arrangement." His eyes moved down the length of her body and she knew exactly what it was he was suggesting.

She didn't respond, knowing her eyes spoke to her anger. "Here, over the operating table, what would be more appropriate and exciting?" He stepped closer and his hand found its way to her waist, then lower.

Anne jerked back, but Doctor Godwin pulled her back into him. His body pressed into hers. Anne turned away from him, his breath hot on her cheek. "You keep your job and I get what I've wanted for some time." He kissed her neck, fondling her chest. Anne reached for a scalpel and without hesitation, stuck the sharp end into Doctor Godwin's neck.

He let go of her and fell to the sawdust floor. There were no words, only a look of disbelief. Blood gushed from the wound; each pump of the racing heart brought more. Within minutes, Doctor Godwin had bled out onto the theater floor and Anne had a bigger mess to tend to.

She looked at the deceased doctor with little care. He was a pig, a bother to her and had no business treating her as he did. She had, however, just killed a prominent surgeon. No one would believe her claim. A theater maid accosted by a doctor of his stature. The elite and a maid who lived in a flat in Whitechapel? No, never.

Anne knew what she needed to do, and the theater offered the tools to make it happen. She grabbed a scalpel, saw, and bone breaker. She also pulled a wicker basket close to dump the body parts in. She was glad she had an early start and had no intentions of cleaning the theater. She would not be returning.

She was calm and rather fascinated by the pool of blood that gathered around Doctor Godwin. She knelt with her instruments and dipped two fingers into the blood. The dark crimson was still warm, and quite fluid, yet had already begun to coagulate. She brought her fingers to her mouth and placed them on her tongue. She closed her lips and slowly took in the warmth and flavor of the blood. To taste it still warm was something new for her. She found the metallic aftertaste quite appealing.

As she picked and sawed Doctor Godwin apart, dinner came to mind. She would dispose of his limbs, sawing through the joints and using the bone breaker so she could fold the limbs into the basket and drag them down to the lower level to dispose of them. For his torso, she did the same, but not before removing a kidney, part of his lung, and a sliver of heart. Lastly, his head. She desired the taste of eye, something she only was able to eat on rare occasions. She removed both by breaking the orbital bone, allowing the eye to be plucked and cut from the skull with ease.

She also took a piece of tongue. Slicing through the organ from tip to the back of the mouth, she took a heavy piece from the center. She gutted his torso, placed the organs in the basket and made another trip to the lower level. She returned for the head and then the torso, which proved to be a challenge, but she was able to complete the disposal. She included her gloves and gown in the final burn.

She returned to the upper level and put the kidney, lung, tongue and eyes into the basin. She washed them well before wrapping them in linen and placing them in her bag. Before she left, she scanned the theater once more. It would be the last time she did. It was a mess and later there would be chaos, but this time, she wouldn't be a part of it.

She stepped out into the crisp early morning, welcoming the mist and chill. The heavy work tonight was more than she was accustomed to. She walked briskly, her normal rhythmic clatter was quick, allowing no time to take in the beauty of Whitechapel.

She reached the path to her flat as Aaron approached.

"Perfect," he said as he caught her eye.

"Yes," Anne said breathlessly.

They both walked up the path in their usual comfortable silence. They reached their building and Anne turned to Aaron. "Will you give me thirty minutes to prepare?"

"Right."

Anne entered quickly and stoked the oven fire. Then she hurried to her bedroom to freshen up. Her thoughts were consumed by dinner and where she would go from Whitechapel. They would not come looking for her for some time and simply to question Doctor Godwin's absence. Eventually, however, there would be a deeper inquiry.

She removed her bonnet, ran a brush through her hair and pinned it back. She washed and powdered her face, then went to the kitchen. She pulled out the meat, sliced everything into small bite-sized pieces, and placed them all in a cast iron skillet.

Aaron arrived just as she removed the skillet from the stove. She answered the door. and greeted him. He wore a fine white shirt, a gentleman's slacks, and black boots. It struck her how proper and refined he dressed for someone who was just a barber.

"Welcome." Anne stepped aside to allow Aaron to enter.

"Oh my, the aroma is heavenly," he commented before turning to Anne. "And you look as smart as ever."

Anne chuckled, instinctively reaching for his hand and leading him to the dining table. She waited for him to sit and offered him a cup of ale. He obliged and she prepared for dinner. She added eggs to the cast iron skillet and placed it back on the stovetop. They engaged in a bit of small talk then when the egg was cooked, she spooned a helping onto two platters.

She joined him, waiting for him to take a bite, hopeful his reaction would be favorable.

Aaron took a bite and proceeded to gush over the meal. "What is this meat? It's so rich and fanciful."

Anne smiled, quite pleased. "It's a family secret."

"Come now."

Anne leaned in. "If I told you, I'd have to kill you."

They both laughed and Aaron held up his hands to concede.

Their time went on like this, learning a little more about each other. He spoke of his early days in Poland and his desire to move west once he was old enough. Where he learned his skills as a barber and the trials of owning a shop in Whitechapel.

Anne went on about her love for the operating theater and her penchant for foggy, early morning strolls home from work. A few times, Aaron asked her if she was all right, as her thoughts wandered. She let on nothing, and even though she felt as if she could, she kept her guard up.

After dinner, they sat together on her settee, and soon she found their distance became more intimate. Their hands met and soon Aaron was pressed against her much like Doctor Godwin. However, this was different. She returned his advances, willing to let him touch her unlike any man had done before. She let herself relax in his embrace.

⚜

Anne woke facing Aaron.

He was awake and had been watching her sleep. He seemed concerned. "Good morning."

Anne smiled to reassure him. "Good morning."

"That look from last night is still above your brow - you're worried about something. I'm a good listener if you're willing to tell me."

Anne laid back facing the ceiling. "I must look dreadful," she remarked. She hadn't done her nightly blood mask routine.

Aaron propped himself up on his elbow. "No, you are radiantly beautiful, as you always are."

"Tell me about your accent and I will tell you about my worry."

"Okay." He laid back and looked up at the ceiling as she did. "It is Polish. I am a Polish immigrant. Back home offered little opportunity and England offered so much more. So, I brought my trade here to

191

Whitechapel."

"Polish. I never would have guessed. It must have been frightening to move so far from home."

"Not at all. Is Whitechapel your home?" he asked, rubbing his gruff chin.

"Dorsett, England."

"But you moved."

"Yes, but still, it was out of the country and into the unfamiliar city. It was scary for me." Anne folded her hands over her stomach.

"I can see that. For me, it is natural. I enjoy the change. Even back home in Poland, I roamed about." He sat up in bed, letting the linens modestly cover his lower half. "Is this what troubles you, a move?"

Anne sat up as well, pushing herself against the headboard. She was a little less modest, leaving the linens only over her lower half. "Part of it, yes."

She paused.

"Yes?" Aaron inquired. His brow softened, as if he was genuinely concerned for her.

"I may be in a spot of trouble," she began. The sun sent rays between the small slit were her curtains met. By now, the theater operators must be frantic, trying to figure out why the theater was in shambles and where their star doctor was.

She thought for a moment, it could have been anyone, he flirts with all the wives. Maybe one of their husbands killed him. Or perhaps he ran off with some young harlot to start a new life away from his bag of a wife. It didn't matter, someone would come knocking at her door and she was terrible at telling lies. She has been, even as a child, and her truth would get her in trouble before her lies.

Aaron touched her shoulder. "It's fine. I am still a stranger."

"No." Anne sat up a bit higher and drew her knees to her chest. "It's my work. I'm afraid I've done something bad, and I will not only lose my job, but may also be in trouble with the law."

"I see."

"You think I am horrible." Anne moved from the bed and donned her gown.

"Not at all." Aaron stood, grabbed his slacks, and put them on before comforting Anne. "I was just surprised; you are so gentle and sweet."

"Looks," she said with a raised brow.

He held her, his hand moving in a small circle on her back. "Truth be told, I too am in a spot of trouble with the law."

"I've noticed the one constable that happens by."

Aaron let go of Anne, and she took his hand and led him into the sitting room. "He's rude and loud."

Aaron laughed. "He is. And still, you have me over and …"

"Yes, I'm not worried. You are always so kind to me. That is all I need to know." Anne assured him. "Now, sit and I will make some breakfast.

Aaron sat at the table. Anne filled two bowls of cold oats with a small bit of milk.

"So, you are thinking of moving away?" he asked her.

"Yes, I have to do something," Anne said before she took a bite.

"Then let us go, we can be fugitives together." he said, taking a spoonful.

"Don't be daft."

Aaron took another spoonful. "Not at all. We could travel together. I will keep you safe and we can leave our troubles behind and start new."

Anne set down her spoon. "I don't know."

"Ah. Just a suggestion. It's fine, really." Aaron's voice carried his disappointment.

Anne felt a pang of guilt. At least hear him out, she thought.

"Where would we go?"

Aaron's mood immediately shifted. "America. There is a ship that sets sail soon. We could board it and be immigrants in the new world. New York." The excitement in his voice was evident, but Anne was afraid.

"America?"

Aaron stood. "I need to retrieve a few items from my shop. Give it some thought and if you want to join me, come to my flat at dusk. We can travel at night to be safe."

Anne stood and walked Aaron to the door.

He lifted her chin to gaze into her eyes. She felt safe in them, despite her trepidation. "Do not feel pressured," he said. "You must do what is best for you. Just give it some thought?"

"I will," she promised as she closed the door behind him.

The rest of the day dragged, and every noise sent a start through Anne. She worried that the police would come calling and she would be taken. She had made up her mind after Aaron departed and waited for nightfall. She would take up his offer. She would pack only a small bag, taking very few things, but making certain she had her grandmother's jar.

When she met him that night, and looked once more into his eyes, she knew she had made the right choice.

Into the darkness, the two set off for the New World, the quiet cannibal and the mysterious Polish barber.

The Madness of Hope
Roland Garrety

Thunder crashed, and a moment later, the window of the laboratory was pelted by unceasing rain. Anthony looked up from the
lab bench and scowled at the weather - it'd make the gathering of
tonight's supplies that much more unpleasant. He scratched at his notes,
surrounded by the tools of his trade. His mind whirled as he calculated
the exact volumes he would need for tonight's work, spiraling back to the
greater work he must do on his machine. Without it, anything done this
evening was just a pointless endeavor.

His eyes drifted through the lab towards his machine. It was a
great beast of a thing, filled with glass vials and metal levers. He sighed,
dropped his pen, and walked the length of the poorly lit room. He glided
amongst numerous vials containing preserved specimens, and walked
past the large tank where she resided, awaiting the procedure. He willed
himself not to look at her as he passed. His eyes remained locked on the
machine, and he ran his hands over the smooth, chrome surface. "It's
nearly ready," he said to the room, and the thunder echoed again.

"I just need to get back to that moment to save her. To ensure
the accident doesn't happen." His hands ran over the dials, setting the

195

date without thinking back to the day of the accident, many years ago. "If I'm able to rescue her, then everything will be justified." The cool metal felt wondrous on his hot skin, and he savored it before taking a seat. Unfortunately, the machine was now pointed towards her, and he couldn't stop himself from staring.

His wife laid suspended in preservatives. Her pale skin glowed with each flash of lighting through the windowpanes. Her body had been ravaged by the years and the surgeries he had performed to keep her alive, if it could even be called life at this point. Anthony rose from his machine and walked to the tank. It smelled of things that never should contact a human body in life - formaldehyde chief among them. His long delicate fingers once more reached out to contact inhuman surfaces, this time, the cold glass cube where his wife lay.

He looked down at her face. Her dark hair hung around her, ethereally floating in suspension. He resisted the urge to reach into the solution and cup her face. Her pale white skin reflected the whale oil lamps that hung throughout the laboratory. He glanced to the side at the small system that was monitoring her. Her liver was failing - last week, it had been her pancreas. "The deterioration seems to be increasing in an exponential fashion," he stated to himself as he went to write at the table nearest his wife's tank. His quill paused above the notebook before he continued, "*I am doing what I can to ensure that she survives, but there is little hope for her unless I can get the machine to work or do something more radical to ensure her survival.*"

His eyes traced her body and its labyrinth of scars. He could barely remember which were from the original accident and which were from his continued efforts at life sustaining operations. And yet, even with all the work he had done to her, he saw only the woman he loved. Hands moved of their own accord, and not even the sting of the chemical bath could prevent him from caressing the curve of her cheek. "I will save you, my darling. I will save you."

Zelda had always held his heart in her hands, from the moment he first saw her, lavishly dressed and sitting across from him at the party. Back then he was much more well-kept, nary a scrap of beard across his face, and curly mop of black hair kept tight under the assistance of pomade. He had nearly finished with his work as an apprentice surgeon. He had not yet been granted the esteemed title of "doctor", but he was already known as one of the best in his field. His skill with a knife was unparalleled, and his patients had a better recovery rate than most of his peers. She was discussing literature with one of his contemporaries that she had been matched with (thinking back now, Anthony was surprised he couldn't remember the poor lad's name).

His movements then were not his own, any more than the horrid acts he was committing in her service now - it was as if he was drawn across the room.

"*Travels* was a book that was worth reading, with all of Gulliver's adventures," the young man was saying, "but I just don't understand the newest essay that Swift has written."

Her voice was as smooth as silk and as sweet as honey laced tea, in direct conflict with her response, "My dear sir, do you not agree that we need to make a change to this world and the way the poor and the destitute are preyed upon?"

"Well, yes but..."

"Then surely you agree that Mr. Swift's proposal is indeed of both economical and humanitarian value?"

"I believe I can see the point you are making, but..."

"Yes, why wouldn't you? As a doctor, you're known as one that would advise against the consumption of one so young, but if it serves the greater cause, what of your oath to do no harm? That *is* interesting."

Her wit was dazzling, and the young man left. She watched him walk away and then looked up at Anthony. It was as if the world had stopped around her, and all that was left was her words and her mouth, which was tightly drawn against his possible advance.

"Excuse me, but I believe that *A Modest Proposal* is most accurately compared to the series of essays by Voltaire titled..."

"*Candide*," she interrupted, her French impeccable. "Oh, how I wish more Englishmen were able to respect Voltaire. Honestly, I wish more *Frenchman* respected Voltaire." She paused and looked him over, and he found himself smiling like a fool.

"My name is Anthony, and I'm one of the apprentice surgeons being celebrated today."

"Careful, you'll rub the shine off the good will you just earned with your Voltaire comparison," she warned before reluctantly holding out her gloved hand. "My name is Zelda."

From there, they spent the rest of the evening deep in conversation, and though it flew in the face of every rule of propriety he knew, he walked her home that evening. She lived in a large sweeping manor that eventually became theirs as a wedding present from her father. She had been raised in luxury, but Zelda had never been afraid to work. As he began to practice medicine on his own, she remained willing to help him in any fashion. Their marriage was theirs alone, though they mentioned children to each other in passing, Zelda had never been able to get pregnant. So, it was with relish that she continued to educate herself on any topic popular in society. That was the one thing he had always adored about her, that made him love her more with every passing moment. Zelda could talk circles around any man or woman if she set her mind to it, himself included.

His thoughts were drawn out of his reverie and he looked back down at the angelic woman floating in the middle of a cold laboratory. "I will save you." he repeated, but whether it was for her benefit or his, no one knew.

Later that evening, he drew his hat down over the brim of his forehead, obscuring most of his face. He knew that he would have to be quick about his tasks - she had been growing an increasingly alarming shade of yellow, and he knew that she needed a new liver right away. He approached the prostitute where she stood in the shadows of the alleyway. She was tall and thin, with deep raven-black hair. Her blue eyes shined out from the depths of her face, and her long thin nose led down to delicate lips that hinted at a smile.

"Well, hello there," she said airily, and he noted the reek of burnt opium that clung to her. Whether it was due to an unwashed dress or a visit to the dens earlier, he did not know.

"Hello, madam. What is your price?" he said, and casually flashed several notes in front of her so that she could see he was for real.

"Well, that depends just what you want, my good sir." She seemed to enjoy the fact that their discussion sounded like a high-class business proposal; he found that treating the girls as such was much more successful than being crude. She turned and looked at him, eyeing him slowly.

"You ever been down this way before, sir? I don't think I recognize you."

"No, I'm not from this area. I needed to avoid suspicions."

"Well yes, I understand the need to be… what's the word sir?"

"To have discretion," he supplied, beginning to grow nervous at the length of the transaction. Normally they would be on their way by now, but she seemed hesitant, and he was unsure of how to proceed. He flashed the ring on his hand, and a knowing look came to her eyes.

"Right. It makes sense now. You're high class, but you need to have a roll in the hay with someone who doesn't make you feel quite so dirty." She laughed and he nearly cringed at the sound, which sounded like a crow.

"Right, but we must go soon." He glanced down at the ground and then up at her again, as more of the truth slipped out. "My wife is waiting for me, and she's sick."

He saw the judgement slide across her face for a moment before she hid it away, and Anthony felt himself grow red in the face. He offered his arm, and she hesitated, but took it. No sooner had they taken their first steps, did the rain pick up. Whereas earlier in the night, he had dreaded the rain, he now welcomed its cooling embrace and the way in hid them from prying eyes in the darkness.

"How much further, sir? We'll be soaked through and it'll ruin all the fun," she asked over the roar of the wind.

Did he hear some worry in her voice? Perhaps. He lightly stroked her arm as he replied that it would not be much further. "She was truly beautiful once," he thought to himself, seeing the beauty she may have once been before life pushed her down into the occupation she now inhabited. A light smile had settled on her face, and he found himself wondering at her thoughts. He pushed away his interest quickly and remembered his goal - his wife floating in a tank, her eyes constantly popping open in a way that made him fearful. This one, no matter how beautiful, was nothing more than supplies for his life's love.

As they turned onto his street, she looked up at him, in awe of his residence. "You're a doctor, aren't you? Goodness me, I have never been with a doctor before." Her smile grew devilish as they approached the door to his shop. "Maybe you'll be able to show me all the things you know about a woman's body."

"I can assure you, I know quite a few things about my cargo," he said as he raised the blunt end of the cane he had retrieved from the side of the door. The look on her face terrified him before he slammed the polished brass into her head. She slumped to the ground, and he grabbed her under her arms and backed into his lab. He knew he had precious few moments left. His strength returned to him as he came back into his true home. He lifted her into his arms and carried her to the table.

"I should really see about finding myself an assistant," he said as he looked at his wife. He pondered it for a moment as he bustled through the room, collecting his tools and his chemical concoctions. "Maybe one of those at the insane asylum perhaps? Someone with nothing to lose and everything to gain. Possibly someone with a physical deformity that wouldn't prevent labor." He finally grabbed the large bottle of ether next to him, and took a small whiff, feeling his body relax slightly and his mind expand.

When his wife had first suffered his accident, he had fallen into multiple bottles. Opium, ether, alcohol - anything that he could anesthetize himself with that was within reach. While this only allowed his wife to deteriorate further, and he cursed himself for that, he could not help but think that it gave him what was likely the most crucial of discoveries for the gathering of supplies. He had found that if one inhaled enough ether, it prevented pain. Indeed, that had been his purpose for inhaling it in the first place! But when allowed to slowly inhale over time, her supplies would stay in a state of unconsciousness and seemed to experience very little pain. This allowed him to proceed with the collection process very quickly, without the writhing and squirming that was more common during his apprenticeship.

Anthony often thought about taking this revolution into his normal medical practice, but instead, he hoarded the discovery to himself. He abhorred the rest of the medical community at this point, all of whom had given up on treating his wife, one by one. He gritted his teeth as he grabbed his scalpel and saw. "I'll show them exactly what one can do if given the time. When I rescue her from her accident and bring her back, I'll be applauded as a hero in the medical community."

With the ether placed so that it would be continuously inhaled throughout the operation, he turned to his wife's tank. "Are you ready, darling? Hopefully, this will be one of the last times I have to remove you from this." He began to slowly turn a large crank on the floor, and her body was pushed upward on a great slab. Excess formaldehyde sloshed onto the floor beneath them, but he had eyes only for her. His previous attraction to the prostitute was forgotten, it was only them once more. He caressed each piece of her as it was exposed from the fluid, and lovingly blotting off the excess.

When the job was done, he laid them side by side. He cut off the dress from the supplies, and then clapped his hands once. "Well, sooner begun, sooner done, right Zelda?" he laughed, and the sound echoed around the laboratory, the high-pitched giggle turning into something more sinister as it returned to his ears. And with that, he raised the blade and slowly cut into the prostitute's body.

The skin severed beautifully, peeling around the edges of his knife. His cutting tools were one of the only things from his medical practice that were still in excellent shape. He looked up at the face of the supplies, and noticed an uncomfortable grimace, but nothing more. He shifted the container of ether closer so that it could be inhaled at a greater pace, then went back to his work. He carved his way into her body, dissecting the veins and arteries around the organ of interest. Zelda's last liver had been sourced from another prostitute, and that woman had gone into a cardiac arrest immediately upon its removal. Even now, during the harvest, his mind wondered at the implications of what must take place in order to remove the liver in a manner that did not cause immediate death.

"Possibly something with the heart" he thought as he cut, "maybe even a clamp to prevent further blood flow to the area." He dissected veins until he could lift the liver out and set it on the side of the table in a jar. He looked at it, disgusted. The amount of cirrhosis on the liver was alarming, and he knew that this was a temporary fix at best for Zelda.

He pushed away the table with the supplies in anger and went about cleaning his tools the best as he could. The stack of bloody rags grew higher and higher until finally he approached his wife. He traced the curve of her hip with his finger, unable to resist the thrill of touching her even now. He found the scar from her previous liver surgery and traced it with his finger. Her eyes popped open, and as he looked at them, he found himself wondering once more how much she was capable of thinking.

"Knowing my Zelda, quite a lot, right darling?" he said as he gently pushed her eyelids shut. He raised the knife. There was much less blood here; instead, a sticky substance that was reminiscent of honey ran out of her as he cut deeper and deeper. The smell of the fluid was that of leaves left in a pile during a fall storm - a rich, earthy, wet smell.

He retraced the previous surgical lines, finding a groove and lifting the flap of skin loose. He eyed the veins and blinked repeatedly - how long had it last been since he had slept? Since he had eaten? - and began to cut slowly but methodically to remove the organ. It was a deep black with cirrhosis now, most likely a byproduct of the many chemicals that were sustaining her body. He grabbed it and pulled it aside, flinging it into the empty jar with disgust. He looked up into his wife's face as he placed the liver inside her and began work on her tortured veins. "I will save you, darling." He watched the sludge pour out of her veins and sighed before continuing. "I will save you."

Hours later, he had taken the prostitute to a nearby opium den and left her amongst those that were partaking. "She may live a few hours as her body succumbs to the poison in her blood," he thought, "but I cannot help her." He attempted to banish her from his mind, but there was something about her that kept nagging him. He struggled both externally and internally, fighting the storm that had arisen. There was so much raging inside of him he wasn't certain how much more he could take. Could he really condone his own actions? As a doctor, he had taken oaths to do no harm, and yet he had just abandoned a woman to die lonely, confused, and amongst those too intoxicated to notice.

"If I can get the machine to work, then no more murders will take place," he reminded himself. "In saving her, I'll save all of them."

He went back into the workshop and locked the door behind him. He walked towards his machine, blinking rapidly. It was almost finished! How he had been able to go this far and continue the work was beyond him - Anthony didn't remember doing anything besides the surgery this evening. He sank into the deep, red cushioned seat and marveled at the glass surrounding him. "The work here must have taken hours." The smooth golden levers protruded from the device, tempting him to take them in his hands. He nearly reached out, but he didn't trust himself not to set the destination and take off. Anthony pulled his eyes away from the date he had set and looked back at Zelda, floating in her tank.

Shakily, he used her as an anchor to bring himself back to reality. He closed his eyes and exhaled. The chair became hard against his back and when he opened his eyes, he thought he saw beakers and not the delicate glass vials that contained the instruments for the measurement of the journey. Pressing his eyes closed once more, he dug the heel of his hands into his eyes until he saw stars bursting alight on his eyelids. Anthony stumbled away from the machine and moved to Zelda's tank. He sank his hands into the fluid as he got there, wincing at its bite.

He blinked and saw his wife turning her body towards him. His eyes widened as he saw her mouth open, and suddenly, he doubted himself. She didn't seem to be doing anything except screaming. His own scream rang out, piercing the darkness and reverberating around him. He screamed until the room wavered at its edges, and he fell, hitting his head on the tank.

When he woke up in the morning, his neck was craned at an awkward angle. It was resting against the tank, a stiffness in his back from sleeping at the awkward angle. He yawned and opened his eyes to see his wife's hand floating in front of him. It brought a small smile to his face. "I've been pushing too hard, hm?" He remarked. "Thank you for the reminder to rest." He reached into the tank once more and grasped her hand. He hung for a moment in the sweet serenity of holding his wife's hand.

Anthony was pulled from the quiet romance by the sound of a voice outside. He shot to his feet and looked around the shop. He could tell the voice was close, and he wasn't sure what to cover first - the machine (his eyes shot to the corner at its majestic beauty) or his wife. He grabbed the covering for his wife's tank, and, realizing that there was blood on it, looked down in dismay. He had hardly gone through his customary cleaning operations last night. Sighing, he laid the cover over her anyway and started the slow process of lowering her tank.

The sharp rap of a baton on the window made him jump in alarm. "Doctor Hamilton! Are you in there, sir?" Anthony quickly ran a cloth over the cover, attempting to soak up the blood as he saw the shadow behind the door move in agitation. "Sir, we need you to come to the door if you're in there." The handle jiggled from side to side, and Anthony shoved the cloth into a jar and placed it on the shelf as if it belonged there. He looked longingly at the machine in the corner, but he was out of time.

"Sorry, sir, I'll be right there!" He yelled towards the door, and blessedly, the handle stopped moving. He had a split-second thought to continue to tidy but had a feeling that the man at the door wouldn't appreciate further inconvenience. Anthony ran a nervous hand through his hair as he approached the door - he was surely in a state and was worried about the visitor's reaction to the machine in the corner. He steeled himself and opened the door.

A tall man with a clean-shaven face stood there. He was in full uniform, and Anthony's heart sank as he recognized one of the men who had originally responded to Zelda's accident. The man's eyes darted behind Anthony suspiciously before he held out his hand. "Hello, Doctor. I am sorry to interrupt you on so fine a morning as this. We need someone to come down to the station and help us identify what was done to someone."

Anthony feigned surprise. "Oh, anything officer, just let me get my traveling cloak…"

The officer shook his head. "There's no time, sir. She's still alive."

Anthony felt the blood drain from his face, and he nearly lost his composure. Indeed, something of it must have shown because the officer looked at him in alarm. "Don't worry sir. I'm sure you'll be able to do something. She was nearly speaking when I left but seems to be under the influence of some odious substance." The officer's lip turned in a snarl at the statement, and it was almost enough to make Anthony smile. Instead, he replied, "Well, then I must be about it post haste. Give me a moment to gather my things and I'll be headed down to the station."

Anthony made to shut the door, but the officer's club shot out quickly and blocked it. "I'm afraid I must insist on accompanying you, doctor." The officer looked him over again, and Anthony could see the thoughts turning in his mind.

He quickly replied, "Very well, sir. Just give me a few moments to collect my tools and I'll be right out." The officer nodded and removed his club from the door. Anthony shut it and released a deep breath through his nose.

His eyes darted about the room. There his machine sat - its delicate metal curves intricately beckoning him. He began to walk towards it but was broken out of his trance when the officer started whistling outside the door. Anthony shook his head to clear it and threw supplies in a bag. He knew that the longer he delayed, the more likely the prostitute would perish before he got there. He picked up the scalpel he had used to cut her, and as he did, the semblance of a plan formed in his mind. He glanced back at the corner where his machine sat. No - not just a machine, but a *time* machine. He could erase all of this, including anything that happened to the pesky officer that stood outside.

He gripped the scalpel more firmly in his hand and grinned. The grin looked far too large on his gaunt, sunken face.

"My machine will work and undo any of these actions. It will be like they never occurred in the first place," he thought to himself as he walked to the door. He took a deep breath, steeling himself; his plan would work only if the element of surprise remained intact.

"Officer?" he intoned, raising his voice so it would be heard outside. "I wonder if you could help me carry a few items?" He cracked open the door and stepped to the side of its frame, pressing his body against the wall. The officer took the bait and stepped through the door. Anthony lunged at him and slammed the scalpel into the neck of the unsuspecting man. The officer's eyes bulged as blood sprayed from the wound in a fan that coated the ground in front of him. His hands fumbled at his belt, most likely trying to retrieve a weapon to use against Anthony. Anthony walked behind him and shut the door, and then kicked the officer in the back, causing him to stumble to the floor. "No one is going to stop me! No one will be able to keep me from getting her back!" he yelled, as laughter bubbled out of his throat.

The sound was wild and echoed throughout the laboratory, as the officer stopped his movements and sank further to the ground. A gurgling sound was the only noise other than Anthony's laughter. He stood over the officer and brought the scalpel down again and again until he felt it bend against one of the man's bones. He straightened up and wiped the blood from his face. He tossed his weapon to the ground. He wouldn't be needing it anymore.

He moved back to where he had hidden his wife's tank and threw off the covering. "Zelda!" he cried out, emotions taking control of his voice and increasing its volume. He saw her floating in the tank, and once more her eyes popped open. The lifeless, sightless eyes of the near dead. For a moment, his conviction wavered. There was something in those eyes that was much deeper than he understood. He started to turn back to the officer, regret forming in his heart, but his mind rebelled against the action. "The machine," it whispered to him slowly. "The machine, THE machine, THE MACHINE."

"The Machine." he said out loud, and it centered him. He looked once more at his wife's floating body. "I'll see you in a few moments, my darling." His hands reached out, but he knew if he touched her, he'd have an even harder time leaving.

In moments, he was sinking into the soft cushion of the time machine. He set the dates accordingly and ran his hands over it one last time. The fact that he still couldn't remember finishing it nagged at him, but he banished the feeling. He was about to become the first person to move through time. His hands reached out and grabbed the lever that would propel him to the date. He engaged the device, feeling the hum of the machine under him as it began to function. "For you Zelda." he whispered as he fully depressed the lever. A beam of white light shot from the front of the machine and enveloped him totally. The light was warm, and in it, he thought he could hear voices. Thousands and thousands of them, surrounding him and sinking into his body. There was a slight sense that he was being torn apart, most likely a side effect of the time travel process. He closed his eyes and gave himself into it, as he was propelled into the past.

Captain Adamson looked at the officers in front of him. They were good men, strong and receptive to the way he liked to work. But they were clearly uncomfortable being here. His voice, gruff with a heavily pronounced Irish background, rang out. "Men, you're here to do a job. I don't need your opinions or your hearts. Simply give me whatever you can. What happened here is despicable. But keep in mind, the young man has been taken into custody and has been stopped. He is undoubtedly insane." With that, they shuffled off and started to search the home.

He couldn't help but feel the dancing of fingers on his spine as he remembered the events of last week. After Officer Eaglesfield had gone missing when visiting the home of Doctor Hamilton, he had quickly gathered a team and headed to the house. Within moments of getting there, they heard screaming, so they burst into the laboratory. What greeted them was a grisly sight. Officer Eaglesfield was dead on the floor. A woman, later identified as the corpse of the doctor's wife, was floating in a vat of undetermined liquid in the center of the room. And the doctor himself had been found screaming in agony amongst a pile of metal.

Adamson had approached, service weapon at the ready. "Doctor, what happened here?" But the words had no effect on the doctor.

"My MACHINE!" he yelled, barely pausing before hurtling again into that agonizing scream. Adamson's experienced eyes had taken in the mess of dials and knobs that surrounded the doctor on the floor, but none of it made any sense to him. "Doctor, what happened to Officer Eaglesfield?"

At last, the Doctor seemed to come to himself. There was a flash of recognition, and in it, Adamson saw the pain on the young man's face. But then it was gone, and in its place was the beginning of a laugh that was like the most horrible clown Adamson could imagine. The sound bounced around the laboratory and rose in crescendo before the Doctor shouted, "I kept her alive! ME! MY WORK. Don't you dare take her from me." The man had tried to stand but was tangled in wires and fell to the ground, where Adamson motioned for his doctors to take him into custody. But he'd never forget that laugh. He suspected few would - Hamilton still hadn't stopped laughing nearly a week later.

They had recovered dozens of body parts floating in jars around the laboratory. They painted a grim picture, linking numerous women to the doctor. And still they found things that gave them pause. Adamson looked down at the writings recovered from one of the man's journals and read them over once more. The lettering was small and cramped, and at odds with the rest of the handwriting in the journal:

I find that at this point I can scarcely trust myself, due to the fact I enjoy the chase so much. I know that the machine does not work - numerous experiments show that the catalyst I need for the reaction is simply not present at this time (Ha-ha! Indeed, I almost seem to need a time machine to find a way to power it). However, I find that I am unsure if the work I am doing is keeping Zelda alive, or simply allowing me to maintain what shred of sanity I have left. Until then, I will give into the rush. I will continue to kill more and more, for no other reason than I enjoy the act of cutting. Maybe one day I shall find the catalyst and be able to remove my actions, but until then, I will be known only as Jack.

Author Biographies

BRAD ACEVEDO writes out of the alligator infested shores of Gulf Coast Florida. He lives with his wife, a collection of horror memorabilia and way too many pop culture figurines. When not writing, he can be found in the Florida theme parks or braving the woodlands and swamps in search of local lore, haunted locales and the elusive Skunk Ape.

DAVID ANDREWS is an accidental writer who spends his lunch breaks pondering the world so he can create poems by nightfall. An avid sports fan, when he is not writing, he enjoys running and spending time with his family and dogs. This is his first publication.

A horror fan since the time she saw a live birth, R.A. BUSBY spends her time running through the desert with her dog and thinking of weird things to write about.

MARIE CASEY is a writer and mysterious presence, In her past life, she was a timid, cave-dwelling mouse. Now she seeks to experience sunlight in the dream of sharing her thoughts, feelings, and words with the flowers she has admired for years.

A man of many faces, SPYDER COLLINS haunts the caves of Colorado, where he weaves disturbing tales of horror and suffering. When he's not agitating the minds of unsuspecting readers, he pens soul-shattering poetry. Sometimes he does both. His work was featured in the anthology, *Twisted Love*, and he has recently released a poetry collection called *Adrift on a Sea of Shadows*.

ROLAND GARRETY is amongst the many phantasms you may see slinking through graveyards in Missouri. The thing about this specter is that he will almost always be seen with a book. He also enjoys other mundane hobbies like gardening and submerging himself in horror films. Unbeknownst to those closest to him, when the moon is fullest in the sky, he spends his limited free time spinning dark stories and poetry."

REBECCA JONES-HOWE lives in Kamloops, British Columbia. Her work has appeared in PANK, Dark Moon Digest, and in *The New Black* anthology of neo-noir fiction. Her first collection, *Vile Men*, was published in 2015. She frequently blogs about writer life and scathingly reviews V.C. Andrews novels on her website, rebeccajoneshowe.com.

JEREMY MEGARGEE has always loved dark fiction. He cut his teeth on R.L Stine's Goosebumps series as a child and a fascination with Stephen King's work followed later in life. Jeremy weaves his tales of personal horror from Martinsburg, West Virginia with his cat Lazarus acting as his muse/familiar.

NICK PETROU works as a freelance writer out of Perth, Western Australia, where he likes to read unsettling fiction and complain about the sun. His short fiction has appeared or is forthcoming in Ghost Orchid Press, two anthologies by Black Hare Press, and in AntipodeanSF. You can find out everything there is to know about him (and more) at nspetrou.com.

Horror writer and part-time dark goddess, CASSANDRA L. THOMPSON has been creating stories since she got her grubby little hands around a pen. When she is not busy managing a house full of feral children (human and canine), you can find her wandering around cemeteries, taking pictures of abandoned things, or in the library doing research on her latest obsession. She has a B.A. in History and a MLIS, but she ignores her degrees to focus on *The Ancient Ones Trilogy*, manage her horror blog, Tales from the Shadows, and scribe for Hekate for the writing initiative, In the Pantheon. If that's not enough, she is also the founder of Quill & Crow Publishing House. But more often than not, she is simply staring off into space, imaging other worlds and things that go bump in the night.

For more Gothic literature visit
www.quillandcrowpublishinghouse.com

CPSIA information can be obtained
at www.ICGtesting.com
Printed in the USA
LVHW111153060621
689477LV00018B/571